D0070560

Tender Melody

Elizabeth Penney

Annie's®

AnniesFiction.com

Books in The Inn at Magnolia Harbor series

Where Hope Blooms
Safe Harbor
Binding Vows
Tender Melody
At Summer's End
Mending the Past

. . . and more to come!

Library of Congress-in-Publication Data
Tender Melody / by Elizabeth Penney
p. cm.
I. Title
2019902924

AnniesFiction.com
(800) 282-6643
The Inn at Magnolia Harbor™
Series Creator: Shari Lohner
Editor: Lorie Jones
Cover Illustrator: Bonnie Leick

10 11 12 13 14 | Printed in China | 9 8 7 6 5 4 3 2 1

1

Daria

There it was, the last interlude before the finale. Straightening her spine and inhaling to the very bottom of her lungs, Daria Hargreaves focused on the velvet curtains in the back of the room. But she saw nothing. She was aware only of the deep, dramatic notes reverberating in the room and through her body, each nuance perfect under the skilled fingers of her accompanist.

The utter silence from the small audience informed her that they were enthralled, captured by the music, caught up in the spell cast by their performance of a Verdi aria.

It was every performer's dream to wield this power. At age twenty-six, Daria was at the peak of her talent. Her voice had both maturity and control, and she infused the magical ingredient of emotion into each note. If only . . .

A dull pain began to throb at the base of her skull, a result of the accident that had almost claimed her life.

A performer must not allow personal misfortunes or heartache to derail a performance. On the contrary, you must make use of the pain, think of it as a ladder leading you higher. This bracing advice from Madame Fornier, her voice coach, lengthened her spine even more.

Allowing sorrow, regret, and guilt to swirl through her like a stormy tide, Daria opened her mouth and sang. Each lucid note fell like sparkling glass into the still pool of the room.

Applause thundered, echoing in the high-ceilinged room. Cheers and bravos, even stamping feet followed, an extreme show of emotion from this buttoned-up, affluent crowd.

Daria bowed deeply, both hands held out at her sides.

Darryl Hargreaves, her half brother and accompanist, slid off the piano bench to join her in a bow. He clasped her hand too tightly, his glance at her cold despite the broad grin creasing his chiseled, handsome face. Streaks of gray ran through his thick hair, worn swept back and slightly too long, like a lion's mane.

In unison, the siblings dipped their heads, holding the posture for several seconds. Then they raised their heads. Daria accepted flowers and Darryl the congratulations of their hosts.

"That was magnificent," Mildred said, patting her substantial chest, where diamonds glittered. The jewels also sparkled on each finger and shivered down her fleshy arm. "Wasn't it?" She turned to her husband, hovering behind her.

Orville stepped forward and thrust a meaty hand for Darryl to shake, patting him on the shoulder with the other. "Incredible. Well worth the price of admission." He winked.

Daria sensed Darryl's distaste in the rigidity of his wide shoulders. Later, once they were safely away from this fine house, he would complain about Orville and his friends, their selfish wealth and condescending attitudes.

But now Darryl merely smiled, baring his perfect teeth in an infectious grin. "Where would we be without our patrons of the arts?" he murmured. He sent Daria a sideways glance.

She knew that was her cue. She held back a sigh as she accepted Orville's arm. "I'd love to have you accompany me to the buffet," she told her host. "So tell me. What was your favorite piece tonight?"

For the rest of the evening, Daria resolutely kept her attention on the people around her. She listened to hunting stories from out West and in Africa, heard about new art acquisitions and admired some paintings, and tolerated much gossip about people she didn't know and never would. She floated like a rare butterfly among the moneyed group, aware that to them, she was an exotic exhibit proving Mildred and Orville's good taste and cultural refinement.

And gullibility. Late that evening, she and Darryl slid into their rented Cadillac SUV, ready to drive to their next gig somewhere in South Carolina.

Darryl started the engine, which settled into a purring hum. "We did well tonight, little sis." He put an arm across the seat and backed out of the space, then shifted the gear lever to drive forward, the wheels crunching on the gravel.

Daria's belly clenched in a painful knot. He wasn't talking about the performance. "I wish—"

"Wish what?" Darryl stopped the vehicle with a jolt at the end of the drive. Then he turned left so sharply the seat belt cut into Daria's neck. "Wish that our patrons would pay us what we're worth?"

She didn't respond.

His face twisted into a sneer, visible under the passing streetlights. He foraged in his jacket pocket and removed a glittering string of jewels. "You think Mildred will miss these? Not with what she's got stashed away."

With a gasp, Daria sank back against the soft leather seat. She'd known full well what Darryl was going to do, but it still shocked her every time. She tensed, believing that any moment sirens would wail behind them, accompanied by flashing blue lights.

But there was nothing except dark, sleeping mansions set back among lush, landscaped grounds. Yet another upscale neighborhood scheduled on their cross-country tour.

"Besides, they're insured to the hilt. The maid will probably get fired. But no one will suspect the beautiful, talented Daria Paris," Darryl said, using her stage name, "or her handsome accompanist." His hoarse laughter rang out in the enclosed space.

The sound made Daria's head throb. She pressed her fingers into both sides of her forehead, hoping that the migraine wouldn't take hold. Once it did, she would suffer for days. Nausea churned, another symptom, and even the streetlights felt too bright to her sensitive eyes. But she'd soldier through, as did all performers worth their salt.

Besides, she had to. Or else Darryl would carry out his threats. Studying her brother's profile, she knew he was quite capable of doing so. In fact, he was heartless. It was hard to believe they were related, that Papa's first wife had given birth to such a monster.

But Daria was no better. If she weren't also guilty, Darryl would find no foothold to use as leverage. All she could do was hope that he'd soon release her from this diabolical arrangement as he had promised.

"Where are we headed?" she asked, almost dreading the answer. She knew their next victims would be found there.

"To a little town called Magnolia Harbor."

Grace

Chatter and the tinkle of teacups and forks against china filled the Magnolia Harbor Inn dining room. Members of the chamber of commerce had finished their afternoon meeting and were now enjoying refreshments provided by the innkeepers, Grace Porter and her sister, Charlotte Wylde.

"The peach streusel cake is a big hit," Grace whispered to Charlotte, who was slicing a new pan of the treat at the refreshment table.

Harvey Bascombe, the big and burly owner of the hardware and paint store downtown, approached. He carried his empty plate, obviously looking for seconds.

"I think that recipe is going to make the cut," Charlotte responded with a laugh, referring to the new cookbook she was working on. It was called *Comfort and Cheer from Magnolia Harbor Inn*. In addition to cooking for the inn guests, Charlotte wrote best-selling cookbooks. She slid a piece of cake onto Harvey's plate. "Here you go."

"Thank you," Harvey said, smiling.

"I wish I could squeeze in another helping," Julep Buckley said with a toss of her close-cropped curls. The tiny, frail older woman patted her midriff. "But I'm fit to bust." Julep didn't own a business, but the historian was involved with almost every civic group in town. In addition to her volunteer hours, her generous donations were notable.

"Good thing my wife isn't here. She definitely wouldn't approve." Harvey gave a hearty laugh and returned to his seat.

Julep smiled at the sisters. "I wanted to thank you for agreeing to host the last concert of the festival. It's shaping up to be one of the best events we've ever had in town."

The festival would last a week, with concerts by renowned musicians held in various locations around town. Ticket proceeds were slated to support the local school district's music program. Wealthy sponsors and businesses had made the event possible.

"One of the performers is staying here," Grace said. "Daria Paris. And her accompanist, Darryl Hargreaves." Darryl had made the room reservations, and he had a deep, resonant voice and an engaging manner, even over the phone. He'd mentioned that Daria was his sister, calling their working together "a family business."

Julep clasped her hands. "That young woman is wonderful. We were so fortunate to get her. Even though she's a newcomer on the classical music scene, she's already fully booked. I understand Darryl is a talented pianist too."

"I've heard Daria's recordings. She has a gorgeous voice." Charlotte moved on to the cookie platters, consolidating the leftovers. She had made peanut butter chocolate chip, white chocolate chip macadamia nut, and cranberry orange cookies. Leftovers would be put out for the guests of the inn to enjoy.

Dean Bradley approached the table, cake plate in hand. He owned The Tidewater, the small inn and restaurant on the other side of Lake Haven. Dean was also a chef, and he and Charlotte had once been rivals while working in Charleston, South Carolina. Now they had a mostly friendly working relationship, with both inns helping each other out when needed. "I heard a rumor there was more of that scrumptious cake." He smiled. "I'll take another piece and the recipe."

"Yes to the cake, but no to the recipe," Charlotte said as she served Dean. "It's a family secret." Her expression was smug.

"A family recipe?" Dean turned to Grace. "Perhaps you'll be more receptive to my request," he said, thickening his drawl into an incredibly charming Southern accent.

Julep cocked her head and studied Dean. "You're a charmer, make no mistake."

"Never trust a charmer," Charlotte muttered under her breath, giving Dean an innocent smile when he glared at her in mock anger. She and the other chef had a bantering, teasing relationship that added a spark to their frequent interactions. "Sorry, but you'll have to read the book, like everyone else."

"I will. Consider it preordered." Dean took a bite of cake where he stood, forking in a huge piece. He chewed and swallowed, then gave his verdict. "This is amazing."

A tall, handsome man with gray hair sauntered into the room, glancing around. Spotting the group at the refreshment table, he changed course and came their way.

Grace felt her spirits lift at the sight of their neighbor. Retired FBI intelligence analyst Spencer Lewis had bought Blossom Hill Farm nearby, and he was a frequent visitor to the inn. He was also a readily available pair of hands when needed, which was often because the inn was built in 1816. Located on the shores of Lake Haven, the antebellum mansion was a historic property and a treasured landmark in the region.

"Good afternoon, ladies." Spencer nodded. "Dean. I hope I'm not interrupting anything. Winnie said I could come right in."

Grace and Charlotte's aunt, Winnie Bennett, often helped out, and at the moment she was staffing the reception desk. The next round of guests, including Daria, was scheduled to arrive later today.

"No, you're not interrupting a thing," Grace said. "The meeting is over. Please help yourself to refreshments. As you can see, we have tons left."

"Thanks." Spencer studied the array of baked goods.

"I love what you've done with the farm," Julep said to Spencer. "Did I tell you the library has some old photographs of the place? I thought you might like to see them."

"I'd love to," Spencer said, picking up a small plate with a slice of peach cake on it. "Maybe I can get copies made. I'd like to create a picture wall."

The pair wandered over to the table and sat down, chatting about the project.

Meanwhile, the chamber members began to disperse, stopping by to thank Grace and Charlotte. More than once, the sisters told the members to leave their discarded dishes and cups on the table, but many brought them up anyway. Charlotte ran to the kitchen for a bus pan to load the dishes and silverware for transport to the dishwasher.

Finished with his cake, Dean helped them clean up, showing no sign of leaving.

"If you want to hang around, you can wash too," Charlotte said. "It's easy. I'll show you how."

Dean laughed. "I'm well aware of how to run a dishwasher. I've done it more than once when employees don't show up."

Dean's restaurant was a prime attraction in the area, in contrast to the Magnolia Harbor Inn, which generally fed guests only at breakfast and during the evening social hour. Other meals and events were catered, although the sisters had been known to cook for guests or small groups.

Dean checked his watch. "As a matter of fact, I should head over to The Tidewater soon. But I had something to ask you before I go."

"Let's talk in the kitchen." Charlotte started to pick up the tub, but Dean got there first. She allowed him to carry the clanking cargo. "By the way, I found an old hand-crank ice cream maker in the attic. You ever use one of those?"

"Once or twice," Dean answered as they walked away.

Grace collected crumpled cloth napkins and pulled off the tablecloth for washing. Who would have guessed during her high-powered marketing days that she'd enjoy domestic duties? Buying the inn with her sister had been the right move. Now she poured her creative energies into making the beautiful inn a haven for their guests.

"I'd better get home," Julep said, rising from her seat with a slight groan. She nodded at Grace. "Thank you for a lovely afternoon. I'll see you soon." She headed out to the foyer. A few moments later, the sound of Julep's and Winnie's voices drifted into the dining room.

"She's a lovely lady," Spencer said, walking over to Grace. He motioned to the napkins. "Where do these go?"

"The laundry room," Grace said. Carrying the tablecloth, she led the way.

As they passed through the kitchen, they found Charlotte and Dean standing with their heads together, perusing a cookbook.

"I've never heard of lavender ice cream," Charlotte remarked.

"I wonder what it tastes like." Dean rubbed his chin in contemplation.

"Only one way to find out." Charlotte began writing on a piece of paper, making a list.

In the laundry room, Spencer turned to Grace. "Lavender ice cream?" he mouthed, his eyes alight with mischief. He dropped the napkins into a laundry basket, where others already sat.

Grace shrugged as she put the tablecloth into the basket. "That does sound strange, but I'm sure it will be great if Charlotte makes it."

The compressor turned on outside, a familiar sound during the summer. But the blast of air rushing from the vent overhead wasn't cool.

Grace lifted a hand. "Does that air feel cold to you?"

He copied her, then shook his head. "What's the thermostat set on?"

"Same as always." Grace told him the settings. Worry grew. The weather forecast was for hot and humid, with temperatures in the nineties. July in Magnolia Harbor was always steamy, but this year a heat wave was set to break the records.

As a longtime Southern resident, Spencer understood the problem right away. "This isn't the best time for the AC to go out."

"You can say that again." Grace bustled toward the kitchen, Spencer on her heels. "Charlotte, something's wrong with the air-conditioning system."

"Oh no." Charlotte frowned as she glanced up at the vents. "Are you sure?"

Before Grace could answer, Winnie appeared in the doorway with Winston, the inn's lovable shih tzu mix, at her side. Winnie fanned herself with one hand. "It's getting really stuffy in the foyer. Is the AC on?"

Winston panted loudly, as though offering his opinion of the temperature.

"It is," Grace said. "But it's on the blink."

"Do you want me to take a look?" Spencer offered. "At this time of year, it might be hard to get a repairman out here right away."

"He's right. They're swamped," Winnie said. "A friend of mine's system went down a couple of days ago, and the company had to order parts. So she and her husband finally went to the coast to wait out the heat wave." The South Carolina shore was about an hour away.

Grace and Charlotte exchanged concerned glances.

"We can't do that," Grace said. "And I don't want to cancel our guests."

"There's no place for them to go," Charlotte said. "At the meeting, I heard everyone else is booked up, thanks to the music festival and other events."

Grace sighed. "Let's hope the problem is minor." She turned to

Spencer. "Do you mind checking it for us? If we find out what's wrong, that might help move things along." Otherwise, they'd have to wait for a diagnostic visit and then schedule the repairs.

"I'll go with you," Dean said to Spencer. "We've had issues at the inn, so I'm quite familiar with AC systems. Do you know how hot a kitchen gets with gas stoves going at full blast?" His smile was rueful. "More than a hundred degrees."

Charlotte shuddered. "I've been there. Talk about being roasted alive."

The two men left the kitchen, accompanied by Winston, who liked to supervise.

For a moment, the three women looked at each other in consternation.

Then Winnie said, "Worst case, you can use natural air-conditioning." She pointed to the high ceilings, where two fans slowly turned. "This house is built for hot weather."

Grace followed her aunt's gaze, realizing she was right. "Many of the first-floor windows are floor-to-ceiling height. Opening those will help."

"And the guest rooms have French doors," Charlotte put in. "They'll provide a breeze, along with the ceiling fans."

Winnie perched on a stool. "What you do is open the windows at night. Then close them up tight during the day, and pull the drapes to keep the cool air in and the sun out." She turned to Grace. "Do you still have the attic fan?"

Grace nodded. "I think so. We never took it out, did we, Charlotte?"

Charlotte shook her head. "Not that I recall. So do you turn on the fan to draw air through the house?"

Winnie tapped the countertop with the flat of her hand. "Exactly. Switch it on at night, and it will pull in cool air from the open windows. Well, cooler air. This week the temps at night might not drop much."

Grace groaned, bending over and resting her head in her hands. "Of course the system acts up during the hottest days of the year."

"That's always the way, isn't it?" Winnie said. She patted Grace's shoulder. "Don't worry. It'll be okay. We'll get through it."

Charlotte stared at the cookbook with gloom. "But my ice cream might not."

Karen

The first thing Karen Roth noticed when she entered the Magnolia Harbor Inn was the sense of stepping back into history. The foyer, with its white marble floors and wrought iron stair railing, was exquisite.

The second thing she noticed was the distinctly steamy temperature, instead of the blast of frigid air she'd expected. But as someone who had spent the last five years in Africa without air-conditioning, the heat didn't bother her a bit. In fact, it felt like home.

Karen approached the desk, carrying her duffel bag and pulling her suitcase.

"May I help you?" the older woman behind the desk asked. Her hazel eyes sparkled a warm welcome, echoed by the lap of a dog's tongue on Karen's bare ankle.

Karen jumped at the unexpected contact and dropped the duffel bag on the floor. She glanced down and saw an adorable fluffy brown dog regarding her with satisfaction.

"Sorry about that." The woman bustled around the desk and bent to pick up the dog. "Winston knows better than to lick the guests, don't you, boy?" She chucked him under the chin as she carried him back around to her station. "Are you checking in?"

"I am." Karen gathered her wits and moved closer to the counter. "Karen Roth. I'm booked for a week." She trembled at this admission. Seven whole days without any demands or responsibilities stretched ahead like an empty road. Would she be able to stand it?

"And I'm Winnie, aunt to the innkeepers." The woman found Karen's name in the reservations. "You'll be in the Wisteria Loft Suite on the third floor." She slid a key to Karen, then motioned to the duffel bag and suitcase. "Do you need help with those?"

Before Karen could answer, the front door opened to reveal two men. One was in his thirties, about Karen's age, with dark hair and a lean yet muscular build. The other man was older, with a ring of gray hair around an otherwise bald head. He had a fussy, officious air as he nudged his companion through the door. Dressed in identical outfits of polo shirts and jeans, both pulled suitcases, the straps of laptop cases slung across their chests. The younger one held an extra bag, a black tote that concealed something long, like a gun or sporting goods.

"Good afternoon," the young man said. "I'm Luke Demers, and this is Osgood Fellowes. We're here for the astronomy gathering."

Osgood adjusted his tortoiseshell glasses. "Dr. Fellowes," he corrected. He glanced around the spacious room with a shudder. "Is it hot in here, or is it me?"

Winnie frowned. "I'm sorry, but we're having a little issue with the air-conditioning system. Hopefully, it will be fixed shortly."

"We'll be all right," Luke replied. "We aren't going to spend much time sitting inside here at the inn, anyway."

"That's true." Osgood peered down his nose at Winnie. "But I'm not sure this situation is acceptable. I don't like sleeping in warm rooms."

Karen had picked up her luggage and was shuffling toward the stairs. She had to admit to being curious about how the conflict would turn out, so she moved very slowly.

Winnie didn't bat an eyelash. "We can cancel your reservation if you'd prefer to move to another lodging. But I must warn you that everyone else is already booked." She pointed to a poster on a stand. "Magnolia Harbor is hosting a music festival all week."

"I'm not moving," Luke told his companion. "But please feel free if you must. I'll be okay here by myself."

As Karen studied Luke's face, she wondered if she saw hope and relief gleaming in his eyes.

Osgood grumped, rubbing his chin, then said, "I really don't have the time nor the patience to hunt down a room." He stared at Winnie, as though hoping she would offer to take on the task, but she merely continued to smile warmly. Osgood huffed. "I guess I'll stay here."

Luke's shoulders sagged, but he merely said, "Great. Let's check in." He glanced toward Karen, who had now achieved the third step, and gave her a wan smile.

Karen had worked with her share of annoying people, so she smiled back in sympathy. That was one plus to traveling by herself. She didn't have to deal with anyone else if she didn't feel like it.

And right now, the way her head and joints were aching, she definitely wanted to be alone.

Karen woke from a nap a couple of hours later. As she stretched out in the middle of a huge soft bed, watching shadows dance on the walls, she had no idea where she was. Her usual wake-up experience included roosters crowing, tangled mosquito netting, and brilliant sunshine on white canvas.

She was at the Magnolia Harbor Inn in South Carolina. Stateside. Clean, safe, and in a snake-free zone at last.

Karen gazed up at the ceiling fan, its lazy revolutions washing slightly cooler air over her. The room was a beautiful jewel, furnished with carved antique furniture and a fine vintage carpet. There was even a fireplace. French doors stood open to the veranda, allowing her to glimpse a blue lake through thick trees.

She heard . . . nothing. Oh, maybe the hum of a boat on the lake. And birdsong. But the place was deathly still compared to the crowded village she'd recently lived in.

Her phone buzzed on the nightstand, the sound harsh in the quiet room.

She reached for it, knowing who was texting—her older sister. Emma lived in Washington, D.C., with her husband, four children, a dog, and a cat. She had recommended this particular inn to Karen because she'd read a feature on it in a South Carolina travel magazine.

How do you like it? read the text.

It's gorgeous, Karen wrote back.

Told you. Get some R & R, you hear? Hearts mingled with scolding face emoji followed.

When Karen had arrived at Emma's door a few weeks ago, her sister had been unable to hide the shock in her eyes. Karen had suffered from the malaria she and her fellow humanitarian workers had been trying to eradicate, and it showed in her sallow skin, circles under her eyes, and severe weight loss. But Emma had tucked away her dismay and welcomed her sister home.

Karen returned the phone to the nightstand and settled back into the comfortable bed. Round and round went the ceiling fan. But she didn't see it.

Instead, Karen saw mud huts and a busy village street, heard the laughter of beautiful children and the lively music of flutes, drums, and rattles. And remembered the solemn faces of mothers as she explained what the malaria nets could do to save lives.

The agency she'd been with had also launched agricultural and small business programs and supported children's education in that region of West Africa. Joshua—no, she wasn't going to think about him. *No way, never again.*

The agency's goal was to empower the villagers, to give them knowledge to face challenges and build better lives.

How ironic that she couldn't apply this wisdom to herself. She had no idea where she was going from here or what she was going to do next.

Desperate to escape these thoughts, Karen rolled off the bed and stood. The view from the veranda called, stirring half-remembered emotions, so she padded to the French doors and opened them. A small table sat out there, along with a couple of cushioned lounge chairs. Potted plants on the railing and the floor bloomed, giving the tiny space the feeling of an enclosed garden.

Karen collapsed onto one of the chairs with a sigh. From here she had a much wider view of the lake. Sailboats drifted past, white sails billowing, and colorful kayaks made trails across the blue. The gardens below were also worthy of study.

As she watched, a woman with dark hair emerged from the inn and walked across the grass, carrying a basket on one arm. The cute little dog Karen had met earlier followed on the woman's heels.

The woman and Winston went to a rose garden, where she set the basket down. She clipped dead flowers off the bushes, then cut red, white, and pink roses and placed them in her basket.

As Karen regarded the angle of the woman's head, the bright blobs of color, and the dog poking around the bushes, her fingers started to itch. She hadn't felt this urge to paint in years, despite the brilliant colors of Africa and the many gorgeous views.

She wanted to capture the scene's tranquility and beauty, its simplicity of line and color and form.

But as swiftly as the impulse rose, it slipped away. Swamped by waves of exhaustion, she settled back in the chair and closed her eyes.

The shade of the closest tree crept over her as the sun lowered in the sky, and she dozed.

When Karen woke, she was starving, and her neck had a crook in it. She sat up and rubbed the back of her neck, trying to gauge what time it was. The woman and Winston were long gone from the rose garden. The sun hadn't fully set, but darkness was gathering under the trees, and the balmy air held a welcome hint of cooler temperatures to come.

Social hour. Hadn't the information packet on the bureau mentioned that one was held every evening? As if summoned by her thoughts, she saw the men who'd checked in earlier stroll out onto the lawn, holding glasses of wine.

The prospect of food and drink spurred Karen into action. She got off the chair and hurried into the room. Should she take a shower? Glancing at her travel-rumpled linen shell and capris, she decided a shower was definitely in order. She unzipped her suitcase and found a designer sundress that wasn't too badly wrinkled and a pair of Italian leather sandals. Then she ran for the bathroom, which was as charming and comfortable as her bedroom.

Karen was used to the living conditions of a developing country, so plumbing and hot water were decadent luxuries, and she savored every second of the shower. Blow-drying her hair and spraying on light cologne were almost equally indulgent.

Before she left the room, she checked her reflection in the full-length mirror. Who was this woman with the haunted expression in her green eyes, tawny skin deepened by a tropical sun, hair wild and curly and long?

She used to be Karen Roth, PhD, graduate of Cornell University, born and raised in Alexandria, Virginia. Humanitarian worker and engaged to be married.

Now she had no idea.

4

Daria

"Welcome to Magnolia Harbor Inn. You must be Daria Paris."

Daria stopped inside the foyer as an older woman hurried toward her.

The woman beamed at Daria, her eyes filled with warmth and approval. "Aren't you gorgeous? Your picture doesn't do you justice." She gestured to a standing sign, which depicted Daria's face, her silky blonde hair falling over one shoulder.

The music festival had obviously decided to use her image, which both flattered her and made her uneasy. She didn't deserve such accolades and admiration.

"She's speaking to you." Darryl's low but angry voice buzzed in her ear.

Daria forced away her swirling emotions and tuned in.

But the woman turned to a new arrival, a pretty woman in her forties with brown hair and blue eyes, and said with excitement, "They're here."

"Oh, I'm so happy to meet you. I'm Grace Porter, co-owner of the inn." She moved across the floor, her hand extended. "The whole town is thrilled about your upcoming performances."

"That's good to hear," Darryl said. "We had to turn down a gig in New York to take this booking."

Daria knew that wasn't true, and it was rude to boot. She sent him a glare, then shook Grace's hand. "What Darryl means is, we're very happy to be here in this charming town and staying at your beautiful inn." She glanced around, taking in the sweeping staircase, chandeliers, and arched doorways, providing glimpses of opulent rooms.

"The house was built in 1816, so it has seen centuries of history unfold," Grace said. "Its previous owners include descendants of English aristocracy and French Huguenots. My sister and I bought it at auction and turned it into an inn."

"Well, I love it," Daria said. "I'd like to hear more about the history sometime."

"And we'd love to talk about it." Grace ushered the guests toward the desk. "But right now, you need to get checked in. My aunt, Winnie Bennett, will help you."

"Thank you," Daria said.

"I'll be outside at the social if you need me," Grace said to Winnie, then smiled at Daria and Darryl. "You're welcome to join us. Complimentary wine and canapés."

Darryl rubbed his trim midsection. "I could use some grub. It's been a long day."

"We drove all the way from Chicago," Daria said, leaning on the counter.

Darryl stepped on her foot.

"Ow, er, wow, my head hurts." Daria rubbed her forehead to cover up her blunder. She wasn't supposed to give out details about their movements, although anyone searching for her online would easily be able to find a list of concert dates and venues.

Winnie tilted her head, giving her a sympathetic look.

For a brief, gut-twisting moment, Daria was reminded of her beloved grammy. She'd been so nurturing and kind, so ready to believe the best of Daria and her sister, Alexis. Her head injury began to throb at the thought of Alexis. How was she? She needed to find out. If only . . .

"You must be exhausted," Winnie said. "But you'll get a good night's sleep, I'm sure. I've put you in the Dogwood Suite, our finest room."

"How does she rate?" Darryl said with a snort, laughing boisterously. "Oh yeah, she's the star. I'm just her accompanist."

"I wouldn't be where I am today without you." Daria gave Darryl a sweet smile. This was one of the games they played. She soothed his giant, easily wounded ego.

Had her brother been like that all his life? She didn't remember. Until a few months ago, she hadn't seen him since she was three years old and he was eighteen. No wonder she didn't have any memories of him, beyond a tall and looming presence with a deep voice.

He gave a pleased grunt in response to her compliment, a smirk lurking around his lips. "So, where are you sticking me?"

"Mr. Hargreaves," Winnie said, her tone slightly astringent, "you have the Buttercup Suite, which is also very nice. It has a lake view and a private bath, so I'm sure it will meet with your approval." She set two keys on the counter.

"I'm sure it will," Darryl muttered.

"I also want you to know that the music room is available for your rehearsals if you need it," Winnie said, pointing to an open doorway across the way. The bubbly joy was back in her voice. "I'll certainly enjoy listening in on them."

Daria craned her neck to peer at the room, which held a baby grand piano. "We appreciate that, don't we, Darryl?" They often had to rent a rehearsal space, although patrons sometimes made their instruments available.

"Yeah, yeah. Very nice. I'll check the tuning later." Her brother glanced around, obviously impatient to get to his room. "Any bellhops around?" Before Winnie could reply, he answered his own question. "I guess not. I'm it." With a sigh, he grabbed the luggage.

As Daria followed him up the stairs, carrying her makeup case and laptop, she glanced down into the foyer.

Winnie's face was somber, but she gave Daria a warm, encouraging smile. Just like Grammy's.

The suites on the second floor were labeled with cute little signs, and Daria quickly found the Dogwood Suite. Darryl dumped her bags, then carried his own luggage toward his room.

With a feeling of reprieve, she unlocked the door and entered her sanctuary—at least for a week. The suite was spacious and airy, if a trifle warm, and the complementary cream hues of walls, drapes, and linens gave it a restful atmosphere.

After setting her makeup case and laptop bag on the bed, Daria retrieved her suitcase and garment bag. The garment bag held her performance gowns, so she hung it up right away. The suitcase went on a stand, and she unzipped it, eager to shower and change. Rummaging around, she found fresh white pants and a floral print peasant blouse. Those would do.

After a quick shower, she dressed and dried her hair, then applied eyeliner, eye shadow, and mascara. One of the downsides of being a celebrity was that she always had to be perfectly groomed in public. No sweats, ponytails, or makeup-free skin for her.

Darryl rapped his trademark knock on the room door as she was lining her lips with a pale-pink pencil. Pausing, she called, "Come in." She'd unlocked the door after getting dressed, anticipating that he would want to chat.

"Hey," he said, sauntering in. He glanced around. "Not bad. It is a bit bigger than my room."

"Is your room okay?" Daria heard the edge in her voice. How could it not be? The place was gorgeous, and she could tell that Winnie and Grace took pride in caring for it. She picked up her lipstick and took off the cap.

"It's fine." Darryl paced about, looking in the bathroom and out on the veranda. He opened the French doors. "You might want to keep these open. I don't think the AC is working."

Daria tensed. Flaws in their accommodations were somehow always blamed on her. "We'll have to check on that when we go downstairs." She capped the lipstick. "Are you going to the social? I am."

"Yep. I'm just waiting for you." He leafed through the leather booklet on the desk, which held information about the inn and local area. "The final concert is being held here later this week, you know."

She put the tubes, brushes, and compacts back into her makeup bag. "Oh yeah? Good place for it."

Darryl strode across the floor toward her, his footsteps silent on the thick carpet. "The big score might happen here." He spoke as though their thievery was merely something random that occurred, like the weather.

A sharp pang of dismay pierced Daria. She didn't want this gorgeous place and these kind women to be defiled by a crime. "Seriously? Here? Why?" Her voice rose to a squawk.

He put his fingers to his lips. "Keep your voice down. I'm considering a few options. My plans are none of your business."

She threw down the lipstick, which rolled off the vanity table. "Yes, they are. I can't believe you're even thinking about robbing guests where we're staying." She put her hands over her face, devastated by the idea of hurting these sweet people, Winnie especially. It would be like hurting Grammy.

"I'm not kidding," he said, menace filling his voice. "The less you know, the better. I can't have you blowing this for me."

Daria jerked her head up, a jolt of outrage tingling through her body. "What if I turn you in?" She stepped closer. "What if I put a spoke in your wheel?"

"Don't you dare," Darryl said through clenched teeth. "You're as guilty as I am." For a long moment, his eyes bored into hers. "If you know what's good for you—and for Alexis—you'll keep your mouth shut and your mind on the job." He stalked toward the door. "I'll see you downstairs."

He slammed the door behind him.

Daria turned back to the mirror and picked up her brush, running it through her hair with a shaking hand. *Please let this nightmare be over soon.*

5

Charlotte

Charlotte carried a platter of piping hot cheese puffs out onto the veranda, guessing from past guest reactions that they'd be gobbled right up. Oh, how she loved feeding people and enjoyed making them comfortable and happy. That was why owning an inn was the perfect career choice for her.

She glanced at the two men standing on the lawn. Luke and Osgood obviously needed to unwind, to allow Magnolia Harbor Inn to work its magic. The tension arcing between them was almost visible, although Charlotte believed it stemmed mostly from the older man. From his frown as he watched Luke set up a tripod, she could tell he resented Luke.

What was Luke going to do, take night pictures? She had to admit the sun setting over the lake was pretty. It resembled a ball of orange sinking into indigo blue. Maybe it would cool down tonight, although the air was still sultry.

"Who wants cheese puffs?" Charlotte called, setting the platter down. Cut vegetables, dip, rolled-up meats, cheese, and crackers were already in place. Her sister, Grace, was hosting the wine station, offering guests a choice of red or white. They also had water, lemonade, and iced tea.

At her invitation, the man sitting in a rocker pushed himself to his feet. Darryl Hargreaves was quite handsome in a showy way, with that leonine hair and cleft chin. His blue eyes twinkled as he reached for one of the golden treats. "Did you make these yourself?" he asked before popping the whole thing into his mouth.

Charlotte's hackles went up at his patronizing tone. He might as well have added "little lady" to the sentence. But she was an expert at handling obnoxious people of all stripes, thanks to working in the restaurant industry. "I'm glad you like them, Mr. Hargreaves." She busied herself straightening the table. "They're a guest favorite."

"Call me Darryl." He winked. "All my friends do."

Charlotte pressed her lips together and nodded. She'd avoid calling him anything at all, if she could. But she'd be polite, of course. Always.

"Sorry I'm late," said a soft, feminine voice.

Everyone turned to look at Daria Paris, including Karen Roth, who'd been sunk in a peculiar gloom. There was someone who needed the inn's healing touch. Charlotte wasn't nearly as insightful as Winnie or Grace, but she was learning to read the signs of a wounded soul.

Darryl grabbed another cheese puff, chewing angrily as he watched Daria step onto the veranda.

Charlotte wondered what his reaction was about. As far as she knew, Darryl worked for Daria. It was her name in huge type on the posters and programs, and he was merely her accompanist.

Daria had an ethereal beauty, thin and graceful, with yards of swishing blonde hair. Something about the singer oozed vulnerability, and Charlotte felt a twinge of sympathy. Working in an upscale Charleston restaurant, she'd met her share of celebrities. Most were just like anyone else behind their glossy, confident shells.

Right now, Charlotte saw Daria don her shell as she smiled and shook that amazing hair.

"Isn't this nice? Everything looks wonderful." Daria floated toward Grace. "I'd love a glass of white, please."

The men on the lawn went back to their task.

Charlotte realized they were setting up a telescope. She found it fascinating. Wiping her hands on her apron, she went to talk to them.

Luke glanced up from the adjustments he was making on the telescope and smiled at her. "Want to take a peek when we're ready?"

"Sure, but I won't know what I'm looking at besides that," Charlotte admitted, pointing at the crescent moon.

"You're in luck." Luke bent his head and peered through the eyepiece. "Mars, Jupiter, and Saturn are visible tonight."

Charlotte turned to Osgood. "Are you astronomers?"

Osgood swirled the wine in his glass. "Professors of astronomy. At Clemson."

Charlotte nodded. Clemson University was a well-regarded college located several hours northwest of Magnolia Harbor. "What brings you to town?"

Osgood drained his glass. "We're meeting with a special interest group, the Alpha Astros. All professors, all renowned in our field."

"No ego there," Luke muttered. He stepped aside and gestured to Charlotte. "It's all yours."

Karen joined them. "Can I look after Charlotte's done?"

"Of course," Luke said. "We set this up for everyone."

"For the laypeople among us," Osgood corrected with a chuckle. "The equipment we professionals use is a wee bit larger."

Charlotte resisted the urge to roll her eyes at his pomposity. Instead, she bent to the viewfinder. Saturn and its rings were clearly visible. She sucked in a breath at its aloof beauty. "I've always wanted to see Saturn. It's the coolest planet."

"Many people feel that way," Luke said. "I'll never forget the first time I saw it with my new Christmas telescope. That lit a fire that's never gone out." His handsome features warmed with remembered joy.

Karen watched him with wide eyes. "I can tell you love your work. What I'm curious about is how the sky is different here from other places."

"Like where?" Osgood asked, eagerness in his voice. He tapped his temple. "I think I've got the world's sky charts memorized."

Karen shifted, crossing her bare arms across her chest as if she were chilly. But the temperature was still in the eighties, even with the sun going down. "I spent the last five years in West Africa," she said and named the country.

Luke whistled. "A different continent and hemisphere. Go, Osgood." He made a ticking sound like a clock in a contest.

Osgood sent his colleague an annoyed look before giving an overview of the differences in the sky above and below the equator, especially in relation to the poles.

Leaving them to it, Charlotte excused herself and went back to the veranda. "That was neat," she told her sister. "You should take a peek."

Grace finished mopping up stray water around the ice tubs. "Maybe I will." She poured herself a glass of wine. "Want one?"

Charlotte checked the guests. All seemed fine for the moment. Most of them were clustered around the telescope, which was proving to be a huge hit. "Sure. Why not?" After a busy day, it would feel good to sit down and relax.

The sisters sat in adjacent wicker rockers, gently pushing the chairs back and forth with their feet.

"I hope no one is too uncomfortable tonight," Grace said in a low voice. "Spencer said it would be a couple of days before the part for the AC comes in."

"I'm grateful he wants to tackle it," Charlotte said. "Otherwise, it might be over a week before we have air again."

Spencer and Dean had diagnosed the problem as an issue with the compressor. It wasn't difficult to fix, but at this time of year in a heat wave, repairs could take a while to get scheduled.

Grace rocked back with a sigh. "And this heat wave shows no

sign of ending. Why can't we bottle a little of this warmth and save it for January?"

Although winters were generally mild in Magnolia Harbor, there were always a few very cold days, even ice and snow once in a while.

Charlotte laughed. "I wish." Her thoughts turned to her latest culinary project. "What do you think about having a homemade ice cream party with the guests? We can do vanilla and a topping bar." It would be a simple menu to suit a range of tastes. She'd make hot fudge and butterscotch sauce and put out dishes of nuts, fruit, berries, whipped cream, and candy.

"Homemade ice cream sounds divine." Still holding a full glass of wine, Daria wandered over and sat with them. "I haven't had that since I was a little girl."

Winston, lounging nearby, got up and trotted over to settle at Daria's feet. She reached down and patted him, crooning compliments, which he ate up.

"He loves that," Charlotte said. "You're good with dogs."

Daria smiled. "They always seem to like me. No idea why." She gave Winston a final pat. "The one I had as a kid used to follow us everywhere."

"Where did you grow up?" Grace asked politely.

She never pried, Charlotte knew, but she had a way of encouraging guests to open up, if they wanted to.

Apparently, Daria didn't want to. Keeping her gaze fixed straight ahead, she waved a hand. "Oh, here and there." A frown creased her brow.

Grace didn't press. "Well, tell Charlotte your favorite flavor, and I'm sure she'll make it for you." She laughed. "She's on an ice cream kick this week."

"What better time?" Charlotte asked rhetorically. "It's supposed to be another scorcher tomorrow."

Darryl heavily climbed the porch steps and clumped toward them, then lowered himself into a chair, which squeaked in protest. "Early night, Daria? I want to rehearse first thing in the morning. We have that performance at The Tidewater tomorrow night."

Daria rocked for a moment before saying, "Not too early, I hope. Some people might be sleeping in." She glanced at Grace and Charlotte. "Is ten too early?"

"Not at all," Grace said. "Most people are out and about by then."

"Ten it is, then," Daria declared with a tiny smile.

To Charlotte's eyes, Daria's smile held triumph, as if she'd scored a point over her accompanist. What was that all about?

Down on the lawn, Osgood was helping Luke pack up his telescope.

"Give up for the night?" Charlotte called.

"Have to," Luke replied, jabbing a finger at the sky. "Clouds coming in."

Ridiculously excited by the idea of rain, which might cool the air, Charlotte went to the edge of the veranda. Luke was right. Clouds were rapidly overtaking the sky, and their thick, rolling movement heralded a thunderstorm.

A moment later, lightning flickered in the distance, followed by a muffled boom.

"Here it comes," Charlotte cried, exultant. She loved thunderstorms, especially when curled up in a cozy bed with a good book. But then her gaze fell on the platters holding leftovers, the dirty plates and glasses scattered about. She had miles to go before she could sleep. That was the life of an innkeeper.

And she wouldn't trade it for anything.

6

Daria

"Don't do that to me ever again." Darryl's tone was a menacing hiss. "You made me look stupid."

Daria shrank back against the wall, thankful that she and her brother were alone in the hallway on the second floor of the inn. "Sorry," she said, trying to inject a sufficient degree of remorse into her voice. "I was trying to be considerate of the other guests."

"Uh-huh, sure. Don't let it happen again."

She unlocked the door and pushed it open, eager to escape inside, safe from Darryl until morning. Even with her back turned, she felt his gaze boring into her.

The sound of his footsteps retreating released her, and Daria slipped inside, quickly flipping the dead bolt. She leaned against the door, breathless, waiting for the pounding of her heart to subside. Her head injury throbbed again, as it always did when she was tired or stressed. Which was almost all the time, it seemed.

Through the French doors, lightning flickered across the lake. The storm wasn't here yet, but the cold breeze snaking through the open doors announced it would arrive soon.

Daria's gaze fell on the lovely little desk in the corner. On top of the desk were some sheets of stationery and a pen, inviting guests to sit down and attempt that most old-fashioned pursuit, writing a letter.

The blank paper called out to her and drew her over to the desk. She should write Alexis a letter. Her sister probably wasn't on e-mail yet, and her cell phone didn't work, so Daria couldn't text.

Not that a text would suffice for what Daria had to say.

With a sigh, Daria settled in the chair, pulling it close to the desk. The stationery had the inn logo at the top, which was pretty. She shouldn't use one of those pages, though. She didn't want anyone to know where she was.

Some blank second sheets were in the drawer, and she took out one of those. Then she picked up the pen, almost chewed on it but stopped, and tapped it on the desk.

What could Daria tell her sister? Only the most obvious things. She thought about Alexis every day and prayed she was healing. But she could hardly say that Darryl had stopped her from visiting or calling her only sister, her twin, but it was the truth. He'd warned Daria that if she went near the hospital, she'd be arrested. And coward that she was, she'd listened.

I'm so sorry. I pray you can forgive—

Daria stared at the unfinished sentence, willing the right words to emerge from her confused, aching brain.

Then, in a fit of despair and rage and pain, she grabbed the paper and crumpled it into a tight ball. What was she thinking? Alexis would never, ever forgive her. Especially now.

She tossed the ball toward the wastebasket. It bounced on the rim and fell in, a three-pointer, according to the game she and Alexis used to play.

They had been inseparable after their parents died in a car accident and they'd gone to live with Grammy in the Tennessee hills.

Grammy's little white cottage had been modest but clean, the site of many happy memories. But it was the land that surrounded it—deep woods, rocky outcroppings, clear streams, and flower-filled meadows—that Daria had loved most. She and Alexis would wander around for hours, making up stories and undertaking quests, their fluffy dog, Jack, always tagging along with them. The sisters would sit on the highest rock, legs swinging over the yawning drop, and sing. Jack sometimes joined in with a howl, which made them both laugh.

Deep grief twisted like a knife, causing Daria to inhale with a hiss. She squeezed her eyes shut and whimpered. She'd lost so much—Mom, Dad, Grammy, and now her sister.

Moving like someone in a dream, she got ready for bed, changing into a nightgown, washing up, brushing her hair. She opened the French doors even wider, in hopes that the room would cool off during the night, then crawled into the luxurious bed.

The bed was perfect, firm yet soft, with ultra-fine cotton sheets. The fan sent drifts of relatively cool air over her body. And she wasn't hungry or thirsty. As Daria gazed up at the whirling fan, she realized her discomfort was internal. Well, except for the constant ache in her head.

Annoyed at herself, at the perpetual misery she carried instead of appreciating the here and now, she turned on her side with a sigh. She remembered what Grammy had always told her. *In all things, give thanks.*

So Daria tried. She named her blessings, threadbare as they appeared at the moment. God probably wouldn't listen to a sinner like her, but she still asked Him to bless the women of the inn and to heal Alexis.

A tiny seed of hope unfurled. Maybe, just maybe, everything would turn out all right. Daria and Alexis would be reunited. Darryl would go away. And she would be free to sing in the sunshine. The dark shadows would flee . . .

The dream began, as it always did, with Alexis laughing. The two of them were in Daria's car, heading home after a shopping trip.

"Don't worry, little sister." Alexis always called her that, since she had been born first. A whole two minutes. "We'll be fine."

In this version, Alexis was at the wheel, though Daria knew in real life she had been driving.

"But it's starting to snow," Daria told Alexis, and in the way of dreams, the snow became a howling blizzard, and instead of riding on a road, they were traversing fields and woods and mountains, the car slipping and sliding, even flying at times.

"Don't go that way," she told Alexis, who merrily did anyway. This was the worst part, experiencing again the helpless dread that froze her limbs, making her barely able to move. Disaster was coming, and she couldn't stop it—

There was a crash. Daria's eyes flew open. Another crash resounded, echoed by the pounding of her pulse.

She realized two things at the same instant—the thunderstorm was directly overhead, and she'd had *that dream* again. The nightmare about the accident last year, when she and Alexis had crashed into a concrete barrier. An early winter dusk had been falling, and that, along with mingled rain and snow, had made visibility almost nil. In a terrible twist of fate, they had been on the same winding mountain road where their parents had died.

Both of them had been injured in that crumpled car, Alexis much worse than Daria. She'd been sent to a hospital for rehabilitation, and Daria had been released to the supposedly sympathetic care of her long-lost half brother. During Daria's time in the hospital, her accompanist had moved on to another job. So when Darryl turned out be surprisingly talented and offered to accompany her, she had agreed to tour with him.

She'd made a deal with the devil. But it was Daria's own sins that had led her into the snare. In reality, she had been the one who had insisted on the shopping excursion, despite predicted bad weather. She'd wanted to find a dress for a Christmas party they'd been invited to attend.

And she'd been at the wheel, right? So the accident and her sister's injuries were her fault, all her fault.

Thunder boomed again, this time so loud the house shook.

To Daria's ears, the sound was like a judge's gavel banging down.

Guilty. Case closed.

Karen

The next morning, cheerful birdsong and busy chirps in the trees outside her window woke Karen. In Africa, it had been crowing roosters rousing her. She was happy to leave those roosters behind.

Deciding she was too restless to go back to sleep, Karen slipped out of bed and went to the veranda. The sky was a storm-washed blue, gilt-edged clouds in the east heralding the sun. The storm had woken her several times, especially when thunder boomed right overhead.

Maybe today would be cooler, although she sensed a sultry heat beginning to build under a gentle breeze off the lake. The water looked like a placid sheet, barely broken by ripples.

Voices drifted her way, and two kayakers paddled into view.

That was a good idea. Maybe she could borrow one of the kayaks down on the dock. She could head out early before it got too hot.

Karen dressed in nylon shorts and a matching tank top, piled her hair into a bun, and slipped on water sandals. She put on sunscreen, then grabbed a cap to shade her face, her sunglasses, and a water bottle to fill.

Downstairs, the aroma of coffee brewing drew her to the kitchen. Uncertain about trespassing into the innkeepers' domain, she poked her head around the doorjamb.

Charlotte removed a tray of muffins from the oven and set down the hot tin on the stove top. She glanced over at Karen and smiled. "Good morning. Would you care for a cup of coffee?"

Karen took one step into the kitchen. "I'd love some. But what

I really wanted to ask is, can I borrow a kayak? I'd like to go out for a morning paddle."

"Feel free," Charlotte said. "There are life jackets and paddles in the shed. The kayaks are down at the dock." She bent to take out another pan of muffins from the oven. "I can put some coffee in a thermos and give you a couple of blueberry muffins, if you want."

Karen smiled. Breakfast on the water would be perfect. "That sounds great," she said, then brandished her water bottle. "Okay if I fill this in here too?"

"Of course." Charlotte used a toothpick to check the last batch of muffins.

Grace entered the kitchen, Winston at her heels. "Beautiful day. Hopefully, it won't get as hot as yesterday." She turned to Karen. "Did you sleep all right? That thunderstorm woke me up a couple of times."

"Me too." Karen filled her water bottle, then screwed the lid back on. "But other than that, the room is wonderful."

"How do you take your coffee?" Charlotte asked, pouring steaming coffee into a thermos.

"Cream or milk, please," Karen said. "No sugar."

"Karen is going kayaking," Charlotte told her sister.

Karen nodded. "It seemed like a good time to go because the lake is so smooth. Plus, it's relatively cool."

Grace poured coffee into a mug for herself. "It is. You don't want to be out there at noon. You'll bake in an open boat."

"Grace loves kayaking," Charlotte said. "She's our resident expert." The muffins were ready to come out of the baking pan, and she deftly moved most of them to a basket. Two went into a paper sack along with a couple of napkins for Karen.

"I'd stay along the shore," Grace suggested. "Sometimes powerboats don't see kayakers, and they can kick up some pretty big wakes."

"Thanks for the advice." Karen gathered the thermos and the bag, tucking her water bottle under her arm. "And the goodies. I'll see you both later."

"Have fun," Grace called, echoed by Charlotte.

Winston barked, as though to chime in.

Karen went out through the veranda door, cutting across the porch and lawn toward the shore. The kayaks were upside down on the grass, waiting for someone to claim them.

Then she noticed a man turning over a red kayak. He already wore a life jacket, and a paddle lay on the grass nearby.

Her steps faltered. Karen really didn't want to talk to anyone. She simply wanted to get into her boat and go. But then she decided she'd say as little as possible and excuse herself politely. She started walking again.

The man glanced up. It was Luke, the astronomy professor. "Great day for a paddle."

"It is." Karen set down her food and drinks on the grass and regarded the kayaks. She didn't want one that was too wide since those were stable but tiring to paddle. A slim orange one appeared nice and light. She took one end and flipped it over.

"Good choice," Luke said. "Want to go out together?"

Not at all. Karen focused on checking the kayak, trying to decide what to say. Then she made the mistake of glancing at him. His hopeful eyes and engaging grin demolished her defenses. "Okay. I need someone to eat the second muffin."

"Muffin?" His hazel eyes grew even brighter. "Nice." Then his gaze fell on his gold wristwatch. "I'd better not wear this in the water."

Karen studied the timepiece, which appeared valuable and vintage. "I wouldn't if I were you." She thought about the watch slipping off his wrist and vanishing into the murky depths, never to be seen again.

He hesitated, obviously irresolute, then said, "Don't leave without me, okay? I'll be right back."

Waving him off, Karen found a spot on the grass to sit and wait. Reflecting on the situation, she chided herself. She could have easily taken off and had her time alone. But somehow she'd ended up agreeing to Luke's company.

The warning to be careful chimed in her mind. Joshua had been very persistent. In fact, that was one of the traits she'd first noticed. Besides his devastating good looks and brilliant brain, of course. Thanks to Joshua's determination, the program had gotten the support it needed, so it wasn't always a bad thing. But if she'd gone a little slower in the beginning, not allowed him to sweep her off her feet, maybe her heart wouldn't feel like an elephant had stomped on it.

The memory of the village children and their fascination with elephants floated into her mind. They'd feared being crushed by the huge beasts, although the chance of that happening had been mostly imaginary, often used to scare their playmates. But children were like that everywhere. In South Carolina, it was probably bears that worried them.

And here she was, thinking about Africa again. At least her thoughts had been happy after she stopped thinking about Joshua.

Whistling preceded Luke's return, and once he reached her, he picked up one end of her kayak without comment. Together they walked it down to the shore. Then they did the same with his. He helped her locate a paddle and a life jacket in the shed, and after loading up provisions, they pushed off.

The orange kayak cut through the water with ease. Karen barely had to paddle to send it skimming along. As the shoreline—and her problems—receded and she became one with her craft, she felt herself relax. There was nothing but sky and water all around her.

"This is great." Luke grinned, white teeth flashing in his tanned face. "Every time I go out, I think I really should do this more often."

Karen had been thinking the same thing. "Me too. I love it." She dipped her paddle, left and right, then left and right again, making the boat race along.

She edged ahead of Luke, and with a laugh, he fought to catch up. They paddled in tandem, evenly matched, although he was probably holding back. Karen couldn't help but notice that he had serious biceps. Not bad for a guy who spent most of his time in a classroom or peering through a telescope.

After a while, the paddling slowed and they drifted, watching the clouds overhead and the ducks swimming nearby.

"Want to go to town?" Luke asked. He pointed to the lakeside park straight ahead. "We can take a break and have our snack there."

Karen squinted at the park, noticing picnic tables in the shade of massive oaks. "Sure. Let's go." With a laugh, she dug her paddle in again and took off, leaving him in her wake.

At the docks, they pulled the boats up a ramp and onto the grass, where they flipped them over. They shed their life jackets and carried them and the paddles to a nearby picnic table to keep them in reach. No one stole a kayak without a paddle.

Despite the early hour, there was a surprising number of people around. A couple of older men were fishing off the dock, people were walking dogs, and two women were power walking around the perimeter path, fists pumping.

Karen set the thermos and bag of muffins on the table, and they sat on the benches opposite each other. She started to unscrew the thermos top and then halted, a wave of mortification flooding her. "I'm so dumb. There's only one cup."

Why hadn't she gotten another one at the inn? She'd had time.

In one corner of her mind, she knew she was overreacting. But the rest of her was powerless against a tumbling tide of negative thoughts and emotions. Compassion fatigue, the doctor had called it. Karen was either deathly exhausted or on edge, reactions triggered by the most minor aggravations. Recovering from malaria only made her that much more fragile. She was here at the inn to rest, so her mind and body could heal and work properly again.

"No problem." Luke pointed to the visitor's center a short distance away. "Hold on. I'll go see if they have a cup I can use."

While he trotted off across the grass, Karen screwed the lid back on the thermos, then clasped her hands together to stop them from shaking. What had the doctor told her to do when she got like this? Karen patted her pocket for her phone, where she'd made notes. But her phone was at the inn.

Deep breathing. That was one thing she remembered. She closed her eyes and inhaled a long breath. Then she released it and took another.

"A really nice lady at the chamber gave me a mug. Missy something." Luke made the picnic table shake as he settled back down. "What were you doing, praying?"

Karen's cheeks heated at being caught, but thankfully the calmness remained. "No, just some deep breathing. My doctor taught me how to do it." She unscrewed the cap again and poured two equal cups of coffee, which was still steaming hot.

"Interesting." Luke eyed her with curiosity, but he didn't pry. He opened the bag of blueberry muffins and took out the napkins, setting them gently on the table like plates. Then he held out the bag, allowing her to handle her own muffin.

Karen had it halfway to her mouth when he said, "Speaking of praying, mind if I say grace?"

"Not at all." She hastily set the treat down.

Luke's grace was simple, heartfelt, and short. He picked up the muffin and took a big bite. "Did you get the muffins at the inn?"

Karen nodded. "Charlotte made them."

"She's an amazing cook."

"I agree," she said. "The rooms are nice too. I'm on the third floor. It's like being up high in a castle or something."

They chatted for a few minutes about the inn, trading observations.

A blonde woman wearing battered jeans and a simple T-shirt strolled by.

After a moment, Karen recognized Daria Paris. She'd been puzzled by the singer's casual outfit and seeing her out of context this way. She waved, but Daria merely sent her a confused look. Karen glanced down at her shorts. Maybe she appeared different too.

Luke crumpled the muffin paper and tossed it into the bag. "Nice earrings. I like how they catch the light."

Karen reached up and touched one of the gold hammocks. "They were made by a woman I knew in Africa, where I lived." The style was a signature of the Fulani people but much smaller than some of the sizable pairs those gorgeous women wore.

"Do you miss it?" Luke asked, making Karen wonder about the look she'd had on her face.

Did she? Yes, of course. But even the thought of Africa made her tense up in a stress reaction. "I do," she finally said. "A lot. But I got pretty burned out working there for five years. So I won't be going back."

Her pulse was beginning to race. Why had Luke mentioned her work? But she didn't know how to stop him, to divert the conversation. And to be honest, part of her wanted to wallow in the memories, both good and bad. Right now, they were trapped inside, like a corked bottle holding fizzy water. Delving into them felt like surrendering to temptation. She knew it would be bad for her later.

"Humanitarian work?" he asked, sympathy in his eyes. "I have friends who serve overseas. I've heard the stories."

Karen nodded, a familiar sorrow rising into her throat. How could she explain the richness of life in the African countryside? While she was there, the United States and her former life had seemed so far away, almost like a story she'd once read. To her, America had been orderly, paved over, and bland in contrast to the color and vibrancy of her new home. She'd fallen in love with the people, but her work had been a constant battle against poverty and illness. She'd often felt overwhelmed.

"We were distributing malaria nets treated with insecticides. They kill the mosquitos that carry the disease." As a result, the mortality rate had plummeted among the most susceptible group, young children. Karen gave a rueful laugh. "Believe it or not, I got malaria myself. Occupational hazard, I guess."

"That's rough," Luke said. "Is that what brought you back to the States?"

His assumption was logical, but it only led to other topics she didn't want to discuss. Joshua. Her fragile state of mind, as well as body. She knew that her time in Africa was over. "It was the last straw. I was ready to come home anyway."

Luke topped their cups off from the thermos. "So, what's next?"

The million-dollar question everyone asked. Her parents. Her sister. Colleagues and friends. Sometimes strangers, like now. And every time, Karen was confronted with the same black wall of nothingness. She had no idea what was next, couldn't even picture herself moving forward. She couldn't see herself in five minutes, let alone five years.

"I was in that same spot once, but I prayed about it." His smile was easy, his demeanor relaxed. "Everything worked out."

Karen decided that everything in life must be simple for Luke.

No tortured soul there, no sleepless nights and anxiety attacks. No staring into the void with futility jeering in his ears. She'd bet his whole life had been mapped out for him, an obstacle-free yellow brick road leading to a golden future.

With a faint sense of horror, fully aware that she was acting unfairly and destroying a new friendship, she jumped to her feet. "How nice for you," she snarled. "But like everyone else in my world, you have no idea what you're talking about." Anger flaring white-hot, she gathered her things with jerky movements, tossed the empty muffin bag into the trash, and stalked across the grass with the paddle and life jacket.

"Karen, I'm sorry," he called. "Please don't go."

She closed her ears to his pleas. But the memory of his shocked, hurt face remained in her mind's eye.

Ignoring it, she put on the jacket and shoved the boat into the water. She got in and pushed off, rage fueling her muscles. Without glancing back, she paddled away, keeping her gaze on the inn, nestled among the trees in the distance.

Her emotional momentum carried her to the middle of the lake. Panting hard, she submitted to exhaustion, giving her trembling muscles a chance to rest. Glancing over her shoulder, she glimpsed Luke's red kayak still onshore at the park. Good. He hadn't followed her.

She was alone out here, all alone. A shuddering breath went through her body. No one to ask her questions she couldn't answer or exert expectations she couldn't meet.

Small waves gently lifted the craft. A breeze had sprung up with the rising of the sun, alleviating its relentless glare a little. A duck landed nearby, drifting on the waves, then paddling to remain in place.

For some reason, it was the peace of the scene that did her in. Karen began to cry, tears rolling down her face, her mouth contorted in a wail that scared the duck away. Her nose started running, the way it always did. She was not a graceful crier. She cried for Africa, for the poor people suffering. For Joshua and lost love. For herself and her cloudy, unhappy future.

Then she thought of Luke and whispered a prayer. "Help me, please."

8

Charlotte

Charlotte opened all the windows and turned the ceiling fans on high. Without air-conditioning, the kitchen had gotten stifling hot while cooking breakfast. Maybe she should rethink the breakfast menus for the rest of the week and serve only cold foods. But the guests liked sausage, eggs, and bacon, not to mention the homemade biscuits that were a Southern favorite.

"Maybe it's time to revive the idea of a summer kitchen," she told Grace with a laugh. In the old days, homes had another building where they cooked meals during hot weather. After the experience of the past day or so, Charlotte now understood why.

"I hear you." Grace set a basket of flowers on the island and stripped off her gloves. "Spencer said he's going to follow up with the warehouse today and make sure they ship that part."

"I'm so glad we have him in our corner." Charlotte opened the fridge and stood there for a moment enjoying the blast of cool air. Then, thinking of the electric bill, she took out a pitcher of iced tea. "Want a glass of tea?"

"That would be nice." Grace bent to give Winston a treat. "I have a feeling we'll be drinking a lot of cold beverages over the next few days."

Charlotte made a grunt of assent as she retrieved two glasses from the cupboard. She had been scouring her cookbooks and the Internet for beverage ideas, thinking that people would soon get tired of sweet tea and iced coffee. But many Southerners drank sweet tea by the gallon, so maybe variety didn't matter. After adding ice cubes and slices of lemon and serving Grace, Charlotte picked up the other glass. "I'm going to take this out to Winnie."

Grace, who was already busy with a flower arrangement, nodded. She sipped her tea, then waved at Charlotte.

Winnie was working behind the desk this morning, keeping the records up to date. But when Charlotte entered the foyer, she saw that Winnie wasn't there. Voices drifted from the music room, so Charlotte changed direction and went that way.

When she entered the music room, she saw Winnie and Karen Roth perusing the shelves of books, games, puzzles, and other activities they kept for guests.

"How about this?" Winnie asked, taking a paint-by-number kit off the shelf.

Karen stared at the box. "*The Starry Night* by Vincent van Gogh? I didn't know you could do that in paint by number."

"Me neither," Charlotte said. "I thought they were mostly puppies, clowns, and landscapes."

"They're coming out with nice kits nowadays," Winnie said. "I found that one at a yard sale, along with a box of puzzles." She gestured to the stack of puzzles on the shelves, ranging from a hundred pieces to thousands.

Many guests enjoyed doing puzzles in front of the fire during the colder months. Sometimes they set up a group puzzle, and people worked on it whenever they had some spare time.

"Anyway, I'm not trying to interrupt. I have iced tea for you, Winnie." Charlotte handed the glass to her aunt. "And for you, too, if you want, Karen."

"That sounds nice." Karen was still studying the kit. She ran her fingers over the iconic painting. "This seems very appropriate right now, with the astronomers staying here." She nodded. "I'll take it, if that's okay."

"Of course," Winnie said. "That's why I showed it to you. Paint anywhere you like."

"Thank you." Still studying the box, Karen hurried from the room. She appeared to have forgotten about the iced tea.

"Well, that was a big hit," Charlotte said. "How do you do that?" Her aunt always seemed to know what guests needed or wanted, even if they weren't sure themselves.

"I don't know. I just listen and obey." Winnie headed for the door. "I'd better get back to work," she said over her shoulder.

Charlotte returned to her own tasks. Now that breakfast was over, she started planning the evening social. She'd serve cold foods and maybe an assortment of small salad plates. How about beets with goat cheese? And mandarin broccoli slaw. Three-bean salad with chickpeas. Her mind was buzzing with ideas as she bustled into the kitchen.

Then she stopped short in surprise.

Dean was standing at the counter talking to Grace. He glanced up at Charlotte's entrance. "There you are."

"Where did you come from?" she asked. "Do you want some peach tea?" Without waiting for an answer, she poured him a glass.

A beseeching expression crossed his face. "Maybe you can help me."

"I'll try," Charlotte said. This was an anomaly. Independent Dean rarely asked for help. To be honest, he was so competent and organized that he didn't often need it.

"Well, I've got a bit of an issue," Dean began. "My pastry chef is in the hospital."

Charlotte and Grace gasped.

Dean held up a hand. "It's good news. She's having a baby. But she's going out on leave a little earlier than planned." He paused. "And

I have a full house, not to mention a full book of dinner reservations."

Charlotte didn't need more explanation to guess where this was going. "Do you need me to make some desserts for you?"

"If you can." Dean pressed his lips together. "I've got other backup, but they won't be able to give me anything for a few days. They're busy with the music festival too."

"What do you need? Cake, pie, puddings?" Charlotte thought about The Tidewater's menu. In the dessert department, Dean focused on simple dishes with mainstream appeal that were done exceptionally well.

Before Dean could answer, Charlotte said, "Hold on. How about this?" She darted to the freezer, where she removed a tub of ice cream. "I made it yesterday." Charlotte scooped a spoonful and handed him the spoon.

Dean took a bite.

"It's peach vanilla, made with local peaches and fresh vanilla bean," Charlotte said.

"It's superb," he said. "Can you make more? I'll need a couple of gallons."

Charlotte gulped. She'd need a bigger machine, and she'd have to get one delivered from the restaurant supply. "I can, but it won't be today. How about tomorrow?"

"Perfect. As for tonight, we're fairly well stocked, though we could use a chocolate mocha cake." Dean pulled out his phone and started scrolling.

"I'll leave you to it," Grace said, picking up two vases.

Half an hour later, Charlotte had an order list from Dean. It was lengthy but doable for three days' worth of baked goods and ice cream. After he headed back to his inn, she ordered supplies and the ice cream machine.

"I'll have to produce lots and lots of ice cream to make up for overnight delivery," she muttered.

Grace entered the kitchen with a glance at the clock. "Can you believe it? Lunchtime already."

"I just ordered an ice cream maker by express delivery so I can fill Dean's dessert order," Charlotte said, leaning against the counter. Her day had been a whirlwind since she'd gotten up. "But I'm not complaining."

"Why don't you get out of here and take a break?" Grace suggested as she removed lunch fixings from the fridge. "I'll make you a sandwich to eat at home or out on the veranda."

Charlotte lived on the property in the sweetest little cottage ever. But she really didn't feel like being indoors. She thought of the huge old oak down by the water that she often sat under. "Maybe I'll eat by the dock. I can grab a book and a blanket."

The shade of the tree was deep and cool, even on this absolute scorcher of a day. As Charlotte spread the worn plaid blanket on the grass, she remembered the many picnics she and her sister had shared on its soft surface. The grains of sand flying off as she shook it spoke of the blanket's last trip to the beach.

She crawled on top of it and settled with her lunch bag and book. Insects thrummed and whined, and a heat haze rose off the land in the distance. The sky was bleached, almost white now as the heat continued to soar.

A kayak proceeded steadily across the lake, its passenger paddling with steady determination. As it drew closer, Charlotte recognized

Luke Demers, one of their guests. The astronomy professor.

Luke paddled to the shore and climbed out, then dragged the craft up onto the grass, well away from the water, and flipped it over.

Osgood Fellowes marched across the lawn and stopped in front of Luke. "Where have you been?" he snapped.

The other professor rested both hands on his hips. "I went out for a paddle." He jerked his head toward the boat. "Obviously."

Osgood pointed at his wristwatch. "You're late for our meeting."

A look of alarm flitted over Luke's features. He held out both arms, twisting his wrists. "Sorry about that. I didn't take my watch with me. It has sentimental value, and I was afraid to lose it in the water."

With a harrumph, Osgood folded his arms across his chest. "I'll try to reschedule the call. Can you make it in an hour?" His tone implied that Luke was unreliable at best.

"An hour is plenty of time. In the dining room, right?"

"Yes. Grace said we can put the video uplink in there." Osgood turned and stalked across the grass, the tassels on his loafers flopping in time to his beat. *Flop. Flip. Flop.*

Charlotte repressed a laugh. The man was so over-the-top serious that he was inadvertently comical.

But she must not have been quiet enough, because Luke gave the tree a sharp glance. "Is someone there?" His voice lowered. "Or am I just losing my mind?"

"It's me, Charlotte," she said, emerging from the low-hanging foliage. "Sorry. I didn't mean to eavesdrop."

Luke unsnapped the life jacket clasps and shrugged off the jacket. "No problem. I was only getting chewed out by my department head as usual. All in a day's work." He said it lightly, but Charlotte noticed a certain grimness around his lips.

"I've worked for people like that too," she offered. "Head chefs can be mean. And they carry knives."

Luke laughed. "He was bearable until I won an award for my work. Now I can't please him no matter what I do." He picked up the paddle and carried it and the jacket toward the shed.

Charlotte fell into step beside him, sensing he needed a listening ear. This was usually Grace and Winnie's department, but she was getting the hang of it. She didn't say anything else, allowing him to continue the conversation—or not.

"What makes it worse is that I'm up for tenure," Luke said. "Are you aware of that system at colleges?"

"Yes, I've had friends go through it." Tenure meant permanent employment by the institution, so future security and a home in which to teach and carry out research.

Luke sighed. "It's getting harder all the time to get awarded tenure. One requirement is that you publish, meaning your scholarly papers are accepted by a journal of peers. I was so excited when my paper got accepted. If I'd only known how Osgood would react . . ."

"What is your paper about?" Charlotte asked.

Luke set the paddle on a rack and hung the jacket with the others. "The short story is, I made an analysis concerning gravitational waves that set the astronomy community on its ear. Building on the excellent work of distinguished colleagues, of course." He gave her a brief summary of the discovery of these waves, which were caused by bodies accelerating through space. "They make ripples, like when a paddle is pushed through the water."

Charlotte imagined space as a large body of water. "That's fascinating. I've never heard about those."

His laugh was self-deprecating. "Most people haven't. They're very technical and scientific and new, all the things that excite astronomers."

"It's the same everywhere," Charlotte said. "You should see how competitive chefs are." She waited a beat. "That's one reason I don't work in restaurants anymore. I want to make food for the pleasure of it, for people to enjoy. Not to try to best others."

They strolled along the grass, back to the big tree.

"Well, from where I'm standing, you've succeeded," Luke said. "While we were eating your muffins today, Karen and I agreed that your cooking is amazing."

"Thank you."

He tipped his head back, studying the rear of the inn. "What a gorgeous building. It's very special here. Almost timeless."

The peace of the afternoon settled over them—a few quiet chirps in the trees, the buzz of insects, water lapping on the shore. Vibrant beds of perennials and flowering bushes were set here and there on the sweeping lawns, perfectly placed arbors and benches beckoning. If not for the vehicles parked in the rear drive, it could well be a century ago.

"Yes, there's something special about this place," Charlotte said. "Grace and I felt it when we first came to see the property." She hesitated, but the encouraging expression in his eyes urged her on. "We wanted to create a place of respite, a sanctuary where guests could truly relax. Heal, regroup, figure out life, that kind of thing." She laughed, hoping he didn't think she sounded too hokey.

He stroked his chin, a thoughtful look on his face. "I could use a little bit of that myself. Is there anything I need to do?"

Charlotte laughed again. "No, that's the beauty of it. Just breathe deep and enjoy."

"I can handle that," Luke said. "Well, I'd best be off." He rolled his eyes. "Osgood is waiting for me." But despite his groaning words, his shoulders were straight as he strode across the lawn, his head lifted.

The inn was already working its magic. Charlotte was coming to recognize the signs.

9

Daria

"Would you like a refill, dear?" the kindly older woman asked Daria, hovering over her with the coffeepot.

"Yes, I would. Thank you, Julep." Daria smiled in relief at remembering her hostess's name. Daria often found it hard to retain names. She wasn't sure if it was because she met so many new faces or if it was caused by the lingering effects of the accident.

Daria and Darryl were meeting with members of the music festival committee. From the deference shown when Missy Perkins, the flamboyant chamber of commerce director, introduced them, Daria guessed they were all prominent in one way or another.

Glancing around at the fine furniture and antiques in the dining room of Julep's lovely Colonial-style home, Daria guessed her contributions to Magnolia Harbor included financial ones.

Julep continued around the table, next stopping to top off Darryl's cup.

"Thank you, Miss Julep," he said, easily falling into the Southern style of address many people used. "Much obliged." Darryl's smile oozed gallant charm, his usual manner with wealthy older women. For men, he used a hearty, old boys' club persona.

Daria ducked her head and sipped her coffee, sickened by his phoniness. She liked the people in Magnolia Harbor. She had a hard time seeing them as marks, as Darryl called them. "Don't you see your kindness only puts a big old target on your back?" she wanted to scream at them. For a moment, she was tempted to cry out. She had to dig her fingernails painfully into her palms to resist.

Then she thought of poor Alexis, lying still and silent in the hospital bed. Until her sister recovered, Daria couldn't afford to rock the boat. And that meant playing along with Darryl.

"We are so looking forward to the festival," Darryl said. "It was nice of you to put Daria on the poster as the headliner. We're already getting calls from New York. Carnegie Hall."

Daria narrowed her eyes. She was disgusted at the way her brother implied that Carnegie Hall was interested in her.

But the good souls around the table twittered and exclaimed in excitement.

"Well done, Daria." Baxter Smith turned to his wife. "We'll have to get tickets, won't we?"

"That sounds delightful." Beulah patted his veined hand. "We go to New York every year for the shows at Carnegie."

Great. Daria kicked Darryl's ankle under the table. They were only a phone call away from being exposed.

After sending Daria a covert glare, Darryl smiled and said, "Don't buy tickets yet. We're still in negotiations." He gave a deprecating laugh, somehow implying that Carnegie Hall would pay dearly for the privilege of hosting Daria.

"So are we all set for the concert tonight?" Missy asked. She went through the list of tasks and the volunteers assigned to collect tickets, hand out programs, and usher people to their seats. The event was being held at The Tidewater.

A discussion followed regarding the menu, with Atticus Forbes throwing in some last-minute suggestions. As in many committees, the smallest details required the most debate. Daria had noticed that before.

"I'm sorry, Atticus," Julep finally said, bringing her small fist down on the table. "But we've allowed Dean Bradley to make the final decisions on the food."

Atticus subsided with a grumble, and with that final comment, the meeting was adjourned.

Missy jumped to her feet, gathering her materials. "I need to get going. My assistant needs her lunch break."

The chamber of commerce director's announcement led to the attendees breaking into twos and threes as they wandered out.

Daria overheard a discussion of tee times and lunch at the country club. *What a life.* For a moment, Daria's thoughts were tinged with bitterness. Why couldn't she have been born in Magnolia Harbor to one of these wealthy couples instead of in a backwoods hollow in utter poverty? All she'd had were her looks and voice.

Grammy's words floated into her head, like a gentle reproach. *Envy is useless, child. Everyone carries a load of sorrow. Be thankful for what you have, and God will give the increase.*

If only she could pray. But when she tried, it was as though she were choking. How could she thank God when her twin had been terribly injured and it was her fault? She'd have to climb that mountain of guilt first.

"Would you like to see the garden, child?" Julep asked her. "People enjoy my flowers."

Blinking, Daria wrested herself out of her dark thoughts. "I'd love to." She gave the older woman a genuine smile, then turned it up to sugary when she faced her brother. "You can go to the inn if you want. I'll walk back later."

Julep put a soft hand on her arm, the antique diamond rings she wore catching the light. "You don't want to walk in this heat. But there is a shuttle."

"I'll take the shuttle." With her direct gaze, Daria challenged

Darryl to object. She needed to get away from him, even if it was only for a little while.

Darryl finally nodded. "That's fine. But don't forget we're doing a quick rehearsal this afternoon at three." That was his way of keeping her on a tether. He'd only let her freedom extend so far before tugging her back.

"I haven't forgotten," Daria said. "Tonight's performance is very important to me." She knew it was important to him. He hoped to lift a few items from the unsuspecting crowd. It was no accident that many of his targets were older. In many cases, they were both more trusting and less observant.

"Until tonight, then." Darryl took Julep's hand, holding it in both of his. "It's been a pleasure, dear lady. Thank you for opening up your magnificent house this morning."

With a laugh, Julep pulled her hand from his. Was it Daria's imagination, or was that a skeptical look in her eyes? Good for Julep. There weren't many who could resist Darryl's practiced charm.

Darryl took his leave, his deep voice rumbling as he greeted those lingering in the drive. No doubt he'd wangle an invitation to the country club.

"Right this way," Julep said, ushering Daria along. They walked through a long, elegant living room to a cozy screened-in porch. By the stack of magazines next to a wicker chair and ottoman, Daria guessed that Julep spent a lot of time out here.

And she didn't blame her a bit. A large maple shaded the enclosure, which also had a ceiling fan whirring. Through the screen, Daria glimpsed a world of enchantment. Flower beds, fountains, arbors, and benches beckoned to her.

"This isn't the best time of year," Julep said with apology, allowing Daria to climb down the porch steps first. "You should see it in the spring."

Daria slipped on a pair of sunglasses against the glare. "Oh yes, the South in the spring..." She bit her lip, knowing she'd made a mistake. At Darryl's insistence, she did her best to hide her background. He'd created a false biography for her that had her raised in the Northeast and tutored by famous voice coaches, all conveniently passed on, of course.

Julep tilted her head, eyes sharp. "Is that a hint of a drawl I hear in your voice?"

Daria clenched her fists. She'd worked so hard to erase every trace of an accent. "Yes, ma'am. I was raised in Tennessee."

Thankfully, the older woman didn't probe. Instead, she turned Daria's attention to a nearby bush smothered with butterflies. "Isn't that a marvelous sight?" she asked, clasping her hands. "And see? The hummingbirds like buddleia as well."

A pair of small birds darted among the purple flowers.

"I'm guessing that's a butterfly bush," Daria said. She knew it was, but after her first mistake, she was going to play dumb all the way. She allowed Julep to point out other species—hibiscus, lantana, and lilies. The sun was beating hot on their heads, but Daria let her gait slow, her thoughts drift.

An old-fashioned telephone rang shrilly in the house.

"Oh my, that startled me," Julep said, one hand to her chest. "I'm expecting a call." She cocked her head in that endearing way. "Will you please excuse me?"

"Of course. I'd better get back to the inn anyway. I need to rest for tonight." On impulse, Daria hugged the woman briefly. Southerners often hugged, but Daria was out of the habit. "Your garden is beautiful. Thank you for the tour."

"Anytime." Julep was already trotting toward the house. "See you at the performance," she called over her shoulder.

Daria made her way to the garden gate that gave access to the street. As she stepped through the gate, she studied the houses nearby and the curve of the road leading toward downtown. In the distance, the lake glimmered.

For a long moment, she stood and looked around, inhaling the scents of hot tar, flowers, and dust. Cicadas, unseen in the trees and bushes, began their rattling buzz. The familiar sights and sounds of home. Homesickness flooded Daria, like a literal pain in her chest. If only she could stop traveling and get away from Darryl. If only she could settle down in a sweet little town like this and raise a family.

Those were her deepest desires. Not fame, not fortune, especially the ill-gotten variety. Although she loved to sing, the same way the birds loved greeting the dawn. It was their nature. But she could always sing to babies and in the church choir . . .

Scolding herself for foolish dreams, Daria crossed the street and trudged down the sidewalk toward the shuttle stop, marked by a sign. Since she had no idea when the shuttle would arrive, she sat on the bench, grateful for the shade.

All around her, insects whined and hummed, other living creatures driven indoors by the heat. Although she did spot a dog lying prone on cool, shaded concrete in the yard behind her.

The dog raised his head and stared at her, then apparently deciding she was no danger, flopped down again with a huff.

Daria laughed. They were in the dog days of summer all right. Which were called that because of Sirius, the Dog Star, in the constellation Canis Major. Luke had mentioned it last night during the social.

Soon the white van came trundling along from the direction of downtown.

Daria stood, indicating that she wanted to be picked up. As the vehicle slowed, she noticed something dismaying. The festival poster with her picture on it was posted on the side of the van.

Thankful for the sunglasses covering her eyes and the fact that her hair was pinned up, Daria slipped into the van, murmuring, "Magnolia Harbor Inn, please."

The shuttle driver merely nodded, and the scattering of other passengers didn't even glance up.

Daria slid into a seat with relief. *So much for being famous.*

At the inn, she disembarked and began the long walk up the driveway, taking her time. The temperature was rising, and thunderheads massing in the west announced the arrival of more storms later. She was glad. A nice thunderstorm would cool off the air, at least for a while.

Daria reached the veranda at last, using every bit of energy she possessed to climb the steps. Inside the foyer, the air was slightly cooler, moved along by whirring ceiling fans and standing fans. Apparently, the air-conditioning still wasn't fixed.

"Good afternoon," Winnie said. "Hot enough for you?"

The corny remark startled a laugh from Daria. "I'd say yes." She pulled at the neck of her blouse, flapping it. "I'm dripping from walking up the drive. I took the shuttle."

Winnie nodded. "That's a nice service they offer. Especially on a day like this."

Instead of heading straight for the stairs—and a shower—Daria found herself lingering. Winnie reminded her so much of Grammy. Daria decided it was because of Winnie's kind, twinkling eyes.

"Hold on a minute." Winnie bent over and shuffled around behind the counter. "I came across something I thought you might like." A moment later, she gave a small cry of satisfaction. "Here it is."

Daria stepped closer, curious to see what Winnie had for her. It was a small, pale-blue book. Automatically she took the book when Winnie handed it across the counter.

Then Daria almost dropped it, as if the soft leather had burned her fingers. It was a tiny Bible, the kind that held only the Psalms and the New Testament.

Many years ago, Grammy had given her one just like it for Christmas.

10

Grace

A knock sounded on the doorway of the living room. "Um, Grace. Can you help me?"

Grace was tidying up the room. She turned to see Luke standing in the doorway. In contrast to the casual clothing of earlier, he was wearing a nice pair of slacks and a dress shirt. "How can I help you? Is everything all right in your suite?"

He took a step forward. "The room is great." A frown creased his brow. "But I can't find my watch."

"We can check the lost and found," Grace said. Guests often mislaid personal items all over the house and grounds. She considered it an indication that they really did feel at home.

"Let's give it a shot," Luke said.

Grace ushered him to the front desk. She took out the small box behind the counter and saw a road map, one leather driving glove, and a nice pen. "No watch, I'm afraid." She showed him the contents of the box. "Do you remember where you left it?"

Luke shifted from foot to foot, distinctly anxious. "Actually, I do. I ran it up to my room before I went kayaking." He barked a laugh. "I was afraid of losing it."

Concern echoed in Grace's mind. She certainly hadn't taken it when she straightened his room earlier. Neither had Charlotte or Winnie, of course. No, it must have fallen behind a piece of furniture or something got placed on top of it. That had happened before.

"Shall we take another look?" Grace said, leading the way upstairs. "I'm sure it's simply misplaced." With every step, she breathed a prayer they'd find the watch. Missing valuables were an innkeeper's nightmare, affecting not only the guest but the reputation of the inn.

"Another thing," Luke said when they reached his suite. "The door was slightly open when I came up a while ago. I might have left it that way when I went kayaking." He shrugged. "I'm not positive. I was in a hurry."

In a hurry to kayak with Karen. Grace filed that tidbit away as she watched him unlock the door. With every piece of new information, her disquiet grew. Luke's door was unlocked, and his watch was missing.

Grace tried to think of an innocent explanation. Luke's room was connected to Osgood's via a shared bathroom. "Maybe your coworker borrowed it." As soon as the words left her lips, she realized the outlandishness of the suggestion.

"I'll ask him," Luke said, opening the door and standing back so she could enter first. "But it's an heirloom, and he knows how I feel about it."

Grace's heart sank. If it was an heirloom, insurance couldn't fully replace its value. With mounting dread, she stepped into the immaculate room. Not much chance of finding the watch in the chaos of clothing or books. Except for the open, empty suitcase on the stand and the telescope in its case by the window, the room appeared unoccupied.

"I'll go through my luggage again." Luke went to the suitcase and rummaged around in the side pockets and compartments.

Grace peeked under the bed and behind the pillows. She checked the floor behind the drapes and opened every single drawer. The drawers holding clothing she left for Luke to sweep through.

After a few minutes, they both stopped searching and stared at each other.

"It's not here," Luke said. "I keep wanting to check over and over, but it's gone."

Grace paused to gather her thoughts. "I'm not sure what happened to your watch, but I assure you that we will do our best to find it. Of course, you can file an insurance claim with us. We will gladly reimburse you." She winced. "I know you said it was an heirloom . . ."

"There's not much you can do about that," Luke said. "I should have left it at home." He put up a hand when she protested. "Not your problem. I took the risk of wearing it while traveling."

As the pair made their way to the door, Grace said, "If you'll give me a description of the watch, I'll tell Charlotte and Winnie to keep an eye out for it."

"And I'll ask Osgood about it." Luke shut the door and made sure it was locked. After he described the watch, he changed the subject. "Are you going to The Tidewater?"

"I sure am," Grace said. The clock chimed in the hall. "And I'd better go get ready." She rushed downstairs to her private quarters.

The mystery of the watch's whereabouts nagged Grace while she showered and changed. The fact that Luke had found his door open especially bothered her. Had someone slipped in and taken the watch? She knew she and her team were innocent, so that left the other guests. Oh, and the window washers had been working that afternoon. Had one of them—

She cut off the suspicious thoughts. Surely Luke's watch would turn up, probably in an odd place. That was usually the case.

Grace rode over to The Tidewater alone, since Charlotte had gone ahead with test batches of peach vanilla ice cream, peach cobbler, and fudge brownies. Grace's mouth watered at the thought of the ice cream. When the big ice cream maker arrived, Charlotte would be able to make gallons at a time.

A hostess greeted Grace with a warm smile when she entered The Tidewater. "Here for the music event?" she asked, tossing back long, silky hair.

"I am," Grace said. She glanced around, noticing that the place was very busy. Dean certainly had his hands full tonight.

"It's in the main restaurant," the hostess said, pointing. "Go ahead."

"Thanks." Grace walked through the archway, the excited chatter of voices striking her ears.

Two elderly women Grace recognized by sight were seated behind a table holding event information.

"Grace Porter," she said as she approached them.

One of the women nodded and flipped through the list.

"Oh yes," the other one said. "Magnolia Harbor Inn. I tell everyone coming into town to stay there." Then she glanced around, a guilty look on her face. "And here, of course."

"Of course," Grace said with a laugh. "Thanks for the referrals. We appreciate them." She dropped her raffle ticket into the jar, which would be drawn at the end of the week. "Tonight you're going to get a taste of my sister's cooking."

The women obligingly oohed and aahed over the dessert descriptions.

Grace picked up a program and wished them a good night.

Guests were mingling while servers set up the dinner buffet. Grace saw Spencer, standing by the elegant fireplace at one end. She spotted Luke, Osgood, and Karen in the crowd. Daria and Darryl were talking to Julep and other committee members near the grand piano. Missy's red hair waved like a flag in the throng as she made the rounds.

After pausing to grab a sparkling water, Grace made her way through the crowd to Spencer's side.

"Hey, Grace," he said, raising his glass to her. "You look lovely tonight."

Grace wore a pale-blue sleeveless silk dress with a full skirt, one of her favorite summer outfits. She patted her hair with a laugh. "I'm glad I made it here in one piece. It's been a busy day. And a hot one."

Spencer nodded. "Oh, about that. The part for the air conditioner is on its way."

She hadn't planned to bug him about it at a social event, but she was grateful for the update. "Thank you. That's good news." She raised her face to the stream of cool air coming out of the vents above. "In the meantime, I'm enjoying Dean's AC immensely."

"Me too." Spencer smiled. "I might stand here all night."

They chatted about the music festival for a few minutes.

Then Dean welcomed everyone and announced the buffet table was open.

"Want to hold back a minute?" Spencer suggested.

Grace, eyeing the ravenous horde besieging the table, agreed. Charlotte was at one end, supervising servers setting out the pans of peach cobbler and fudge brownies. Tubs of ice cream sat on ice, ready to be scooped.

After the line thinned, Grace and Spencer moved forward to fill their plates. The selection looked delicious. In addition to seafood casserole, there were several salads and roast beef. Grace took a little of everything but skipped the rolls, even though they were fresh from the oven.

"You put on a nice spread," she told Dean, who was standing nearby with Charlotte and watching over the food service. She glanced at her full plate and laughed. "I hope I'll have room for dessert."

"You'd better." Charlotte rolled her eyes dramatically. "I slaved over a hot oven today. I sure hope the AC is fixed before I melt into a puddle."

"The part is coming," Spencer assured her. After greeting Dean, he turned to Grace. "Want to sit over there?" He gestured toward a table with two empty seats.

Grace saw Luke and Osgood sitting there with several colleagues. Not wanting to be reminded of Luke's missing watch, she scanned the other tables, but none of them had two seats left. "Yes, let's."

The astronomy professors greeted them as they approached.

"Nice to see you again," one man said. He had attended a meeting at the inn, as had the others.

"Same here," Grace said. She introduced Spencer and sat down, reminding herself that these men were potential future guests or referrals. She needed to put aside her embarrassment and concern about Luke's missing watch for now.

The men returned to their conversation.

Grace quickly gathered that it was shop talk. She could barely follow the technical terms they used.

"Okay, fellows," Luke finally said when one of his colleagues wound down. "We're boring a couple of laypeople to death."

"No, I'm fascinated," Spencer said. After sending Grace a covert smile, he proceeded to ask an intelligent question about one of the huge space telescopes.

Luke started to answer, but he was tromped on by Osgood. Luke pressed his lips together in annoyance but politely gave way.

As Osgood droned on while Luke focused on his dinner, Grace got a good view of the dynamics. She had experienced this type of rivalry in the marketing industry, so she sympathized with Luke.

"Up for tenure?" Spencer asked Luke when the other professors were storming the dessert table.

Luke laughed as he set his napkin on the table. "How did you guess? Yes, Osgood is my department head. And to be fair, a leader in his field."

"Good leaders make room at the top," Spencer said. "I spent a couple of decades in a government agency." He rolled his eyes. "Need I say more?"

Luke smiled.

After dessert—Grace limited herself to a small helping of cobbler and ice cream due to fullness—the tables were cleared of dishes and the lights dimmed. According to the program, there were three acts tonight. After a string quartet, Daria and Darryl would perform. Then a classical pianist would conclude the event.

Grace sat back in the comfortable chair, which had a padded back and seat, and allowed the soothing strains of Bach to wash over her. Beside her, Spencer appeared to listen intently, his profile etched in the dim light. Music was something they had in common, both enjoying a wide range of genres.

After several selections, the quartet bowed to great applause and exited.

Now Daria was up. Grace had heard her rehearsing in the music room, but this was something else entirely.

Even before she started singing, Daria radiated poise and power. People shifted in their seats, attentive. Then she opened her mouth, and they were her captives.

Grace and Spencer exchanged smiles. They were in the presence of true talent, a marvelous gift. Daria carried them to the heights, swept them low to the depths, and then up again, to victory. At least that was how it felt to Grace.

Applause was thunderous, despite the relatively small size of the crowd. A few men even stamped their feet.

"Bravo," Julep called.

Daria's pale cheeks were flushed, her eyes grateful, as she bowed and bowed again.

Bowing beside her, Darryl grinned, his own gestures showy, as though he were responsible for his sister's abilities.

At last the clapping stopped and the performers left the stage area and joined the audience.

The last performer, a petite Asian woman, stepped up to the piano. Ann Lui bowed, then slid onto the bench. "Well, that's a tough act to follow."

Everyone laughed at her remark.

Miss Lui's performance was exquisite, and the applause she received was almost equal to that for Daria.

After the acclaim died down, Dean strode to the front of the room. "Thank you for coming, everyone. You're more than welcome to linger for coffee and another helping of dessert."

The suggestion was met by good-natured groans.

"I'm going to give the floor to Julep Buckley," Dean said. "She'll tell us about the musical performances coming up."

Julep stood with a smile, ready to come forward. Then she gasped and put a hand to her neck. "My necklace. It's gone!"

Murmurs of concern and shock rippled through the crowd.

"She has it." A woman pointed at Karen. "I saw her lean toward Julep."

Karen leaped to her feet, her face flaming. She put both hands to her cheeks. "Yes, when I gave her back her program."

"That's right. She did," Julep confirmed. "Let's not create a riot here. Help me look for it. The necklace has a loose clasp." She pushed back her chair and lifted the tablecloth, trying to see underneath.

Her tablemates began to help, crawling around on the floor and searching the carpet nearby.

Seeing that Julep was busy, Atticus took the floor. "Hello, everyone. The next performance is—"

His voice was drowned out by general chatter and movement.

After a moment, Atticus shrugged and tootled off toward the coffee urn.

Grace sidled over to Karen. "I'm so sorry that happened," she whispered.

Karen pursed her lips. "It was pretty embarrassing. But I'm not too worried about it." She patted her arms and pockets. "They can check me if they want."

Dean joined them, and he also apologized for his guest's rudeness.

Grace introduced Karen to Dean.

"How are you liking the inn?" he asked, his eyes twinkling. "If Grace and Charlotte aren't treating you right, I can find room for you here."

Charlotte, who had been sitting nearby, feigned great annoyance. "Stealing our guests now, are you? You'd better watch out, or I won't make you any more ice cream." She folded her arms and tapped one foot.

Dean put a hand to his head. "Oh no. That would be a tragedy."

To Grace's relief, Karen smiled at their banter. "I'm about ready to head back to the inn," Grace told her. "Do you need a ride?"

"I'm all set," Karen said. "I brought my car." A blank expression fell over her face, replacing the humor that had been dancing in her eyes.

Grace turned to see Luke approaching. What was that about? Last she knew, the pair had gone kayaking together.

"I wanted to say good night," Luke said to Grace, then gave Karen a wary glance. "See you back at the inn."

"See you there," Grace said. "Winnie is putting out milk and cookies." After he strode off, she turned to check Julep's progress. Judging by the distress and confusion at her table, she guessed they hadn't found the necklace.

Dean excused himself and went over to talk to Julep.

Snatches of the conversation drifted to Grace's ears, reminding her of the incident with Luke earlier that evening. A watch and now a necklace were missing.

What was going on in Magnolia Harbor?

11

Karen

Karen exited The Tidewater and stepped into the warm night, pausing to dig out her keys. Movement caught her eye, and she turned to see Luke rising from a rocking chair. "Hey," she said, squeaking out the word past a suddenly tight chest. She was still embarrassed by her outburst earlier. What must he think of her, storming off that way like a child?

But his expression as he strolled along the porch was open and welcoming. "Great concert, huh?"

"I enjoyed it," she said, still digging for her keys. For some reason her fingers were clumsy, and the keys slipped out of her grasp more than once. "I want to apologize for the way I acted this morning."

"I'm sorry too." Luke gazed up at the stars. Even with the lights from The Tidewater diluting the darkness, the Milky Way was visible. "Nice night for a walk."

Karen jingled her keys, ready to find her car and hop in. But instead she found herself saying, "Is that an invitation?"

"I suppose it is," he replied.

She smiled. "I'd like that."

"They're serving round two of dessert. Want an ice-cream cone before we go?"

"Instead of milk and cookies at the inn?" Karen laughed. "Sure, I'll take a cone." Charlotte's concoction was delectable, the best she'd ever tasted.

"Milk and cookies will be my third dessert," Luke declared. He headed for the door at a trot, perhaps worried that Karen would change her mind.

She thought about doing so. The soft bed at the inn called to her, as did the desire to curl up in a ball and feel sorry for herself. Instead, she inhaled deeply, trying to push off the temptation to run and hide. It was time to enter the world of the living again, even if she had to drag herself kicking and screaming. That image made her smile.

Ever vigilant, Karen scanned her thoughts for any hint that the panic disorder was lurking, ready to reappear at any moment. For once, she couldn't find it. She was totally at peace.

How odd. She'd forgotten what normal felt like.

A few minutes later, Luke walked through the door, holding up two cones with napkins wrapped around their bases. "Which one?" he asked politely.

She took the smaller cone. "Thanks."

They descended the porch stairs and fell into step, ambling toward the lake. The night was quiet. Around the lake, lights were reflected in the glassy black water.

The freedom of being outside on a warm night shivered over Karen's skin. She'd forgotten how much she enjoyed hanging out with a friend, free from any expectation except that they'd have a good time.

A friend? Karen's steps hitched. She barely knew Luke. In fact, she'd known him only about twenty-four hours. But in that short time, she'd shown more of herself than some people had ever seen. That was unusual.

"Which performance did you like best tonight?" Luke asked.

She could tell that his question was purely a conversation starter. All the way to the lakefront park, they debated the merits of each.

"And to think there are more performances to look forward to," Karen said. "I had no idea this event was going on when I booked a room at the inn."

"Me neither," Luke said. He led the way across the grass to a swing set. "It's a definite bonus." He sat in one of the swings, still eating his cone, and pushed off with long legs.

"Seriously?" Karen asked, laughing. "Are you swinging?"

He shrugged. "Why not? It's fun."

Karen gave an exaggerated sigh. "All right, I'll try it." She sat on the seat and pushed off. He was right. It was fun. Back and forth they went, the chains squeaking. Karen found herself giggling in glee.

"Told you," Luke said with a grin. Then he lowered his voice and stated in a serious tone, "According to government studies, playing on playground equipment has been shown to reduce stress in adults."

Karen giggled some more. "No, it hasn't, silly."

"Are you calling me silly? I'll have you know that I'm a learned professor."

On it went, his foolish banter and her retorts.

By the time Karen slid off the swing, legs shaky with exhaustion, her stomach hurt from laughing so much. *Guess I haven't used those muscles in a while.* "Wow, I'm tired now," she said. She sagged onto the bench of a nearby picnic table.

"Want me to run and get the car?" Luke asked. "That is, if you don't mind taking me back to the inn. Osgood was my ride, and he left already."

Karen scanned the park. Magnolia Harbor was probably safe, but she didn't want to be in the park alone. "Let's rest for a sec, then head back to The Tidewater. And of course you can have a ride."

They sat listening to the water gently lapping the shore, content not to talk for a few minutes.

"What's up with Osgood, anyway?" Karen asked, breaking the silence. "He seems rather overbearing."

Luke leaned back on the bench, running a hand through his hair. "You could say that. Unfortunately, he's my boss."

"Been there," Karen said. Hadn't everyone dealt with an annoying boss at least once? The real mystery was how these inept, unpleasant people got promoted in the first place.

"First World problems, right?" he asked, then winced. He was probably afraid he'd trigger something in her with her Third World experiences.

"It's okay," she said. "Problems are problems. We still have to deal with them."

Luke shifted, seeming to be relieved that she'd let his gaffe go. "Yes, I suppose so. Osgood is standing between me and tenure, which I've been working toward for years. I've checked all the boxes, but that might not be enough."

Karen thought about his situation. She was familiar with the habit of striving, of always trying to prove oneself. It could get exhausting. At this moment, she didn't have to prove a thing to anybody, and it felt great. In the past, she'd always kept moving, afraid of confronting herself in the void.

Now there's an insight. She tagged it mentally for further contemplation.

"You know what, Luke? Maybe if it doesn't happen, then it's not meant to be." At his protest, she held up a hand. "I'm not trying to be glib by throwing platitudes at you. But seriously, you're an intelligent and talented man. Maybe a better opportunity is waiting for you."

"Maybe so," he said after a long moment. "Sometimes you get committed to a path and later find yourself clinging to it for dear life."

She nodded. "That's me to a tee." Another insight. Tonight was full of them. Was it the place? She glanced at Luke. Or was it her new friend?

Back at the inn, most of the windows were dark, so Karen and Luke made sure not to slam the car doors. A light burned on the porch, but the door was locked so Karen used her key.

Luke glanced up the staircase. "Let's say good night here." He smiled. "I had a nice time."

"Me too," Karen said. "See you tomorrow." She climbed the stairs to the third floor, mulling over various scenes from the evening. The concert, the delicious meal, her walk with Luke. The incident with the accusing woman hovered at the edges, but she didn't let the memory in. She hoped they had found Julep's necklace by now.

Inside her room, the ceiling fan whirred. She'd left the French doors open, hoping that as the evening cooled, so would her room. She crossed the floor to gaze at the lake. Maybe she would go fishing with Luke tomorrow, as he had suggested on the ride home. It would be nice to get out on the lake again and enjoy its tranquil beauty.

Realizing she hadn't checked her messages all night, Karen dug in her handbag for her phone. With a sigh of relief, she saw there was nothing, not even from her sister.

She hooked the phone to the charger, sat on the bed, and opened her laptop. Maybe she could download a new novel, something light to read before going to sleep.

Karen automatically opened her e-mail program. There were several new messages since the last time she'd checked. Her fingers hovered over the keys. Did she really want to peek?

Mingled hope and dread warred. A warning chimed in the back of her mind. Karen knew it wasn't a good idea, but she looked anyway.

Her fears were justified. Joshua had e-mailed. Karen knew that was a last resort for him since he hated e-mail. But she'd refused to answer any of his texts or social media messages. In fact, she'd blocked him.

Should she open it? Again, her fingers hesitated, as if they recognized the danger more clearly than she did. Temptation rose over her in a swell, and she clicked.

Joshua was clever. He'd sent pictures of the village children. There was little Elolo with his gap-toothed smile, holding his favorite hen. Speaking of favorites, the seven-year-old had been one of hers. He was smaller than his peers and shy, and she'd boosted his confidence by telling him what his name meant. *God is great.* He'd liked that.

Tearing her eyes away from Elolo and the others, a group of sweet little girls, she read Joshua's message.

Hi, Karen. I hope you're well. We miss you here in the village. Oh, and Elolo has a baby sister. I'll send pictures if you want.

Elolo's mother had been dealing with a difficult pregnancy, but it sounded like she and the baby were fine, thank goodness.

Before she thought about it, Karen wrote back.

Please do. I'm in Magnolia Harbor at a nice inn. Great food. You'd like it.

Best,

Karen

Before she could stop herself, she sent the message.

Then Karen began to shake. Why had she reopened communication with him? She knew all too well how it would go. Soon he'd write back, and she'd write back. And before she knew it, they'd be engaged again.

Joshua was very single-minded, one reason why he was so successful with his mission work. But it wasn't quite so much fun to be one of his goals. She'd met all the requirements—attractive enough, educated, loyal, and most crucially, willing to let him take the lead.

Karen's getting sick and having a nervous collapse hadn't been in Joshua's plans. His lack of true empathy was what had led to her breaking off their engagement. Of course, Joshua was used to winning, so he'd had a problem with it. Half of her believed that if she did go back to him, he'd break up with her just to have the last word.

Sliding off the bed, Karen began to pace. Then she halted. What if she was bothering the people downstairs? But as she stood still in the middle of the room, every nerve vibrated with anxiety. Her belly churned. Her nails dug into her palms.

She was ready to scream.

But that would definitely bother the other guests. She glanced around the room, eager for a distraction. The painting kit, the one Winnie had given her, sat on the credenza, where she'd put it earlier.

Without much thought, Karen charged across the room and opened the box. That was what she could do. She'd paint *The Starry Night* by numbers, even if it was rather sacrilegious for such a masterpiece.

As she cleared space at the desk, she remembered something about *The Starry Night*, perhaps van Gogh's most famous work. The scene depicted the view from the artist's room in a mental hospital.

If it had helped him, maybe it would help her too.

12

Charlotte

Charlotte grunted in dismay when her alarm went off. Was it morning already?

She opened her eyes. Yes, that was dawn peeking around her window shades. Why had she stayed up so late? Oh, that was right. She'd helped Dean search the restaurant for Julep's necklace. Then, at his invitation, she'd stayed through closing for the traditional nightly gathering with the employees.

Charlotte smiled at the memory of the joking, the laughter, the complaints, and the kudos the employees had shared. Dean had a good team. Sometimes she missed the feeling of being part of a well-oiled machine.

But she loved co-owning the inn. She had to get up early every day, but she was the boss of her own kitchen. There weren't any difficult personalities to navigate or managers to please. And she had full control over the menus, which was every chef's dream.

Realizing she'd better get going, boss or not, Charlotte rolled out of bed and stumbled toward the shower.

After dressing and drying her hair, she checked her pockets to be sure she had her phone and other items she needed. Then she glanced around the cottage one last time, opened the back door, and stepped into the fresh morning air.

Dewdrops sparkled on the grass. A pink mist drifted over the placid lake. Birds twittered and hopped about. Charlotte took a deep breath, forcing herself to stop and focus on this moment. Another benefit to living here. Her home was spectacular every season of the year.

In the kitchen, the first order of business was to start the coffee. Soon the savory aroma filled the room, energizing Charlotte as she retrieved items from the refrigerator and pantry. Today she was serving coffee cake, local link sausages, and fluffy scrambled eggs. No one this week had any special dietary needs. Charlotte was happy to accommodate them, but she had to admit that it was easier when everyone could eat the same breakfast.

Grace entered the kitchen. “Good morning.”

“You’re up early,” Charlotte said. Usually she had the first hour or so alone in the kitchen. “Coffee’s ready.”

Grace yawned as she walked over to the coffeepot. “Sorry. I didn’t sleep very well last night.”

“Did the heat get to you?” Charlotte asked with sympathy, feeling a little guilty that the cottage’s cooling system was working fine. She opened a drawer and selected a blue-striped mixing bowl. “I sure hope the AC will be fixed soon.”

“No, it wasn’t the heat,” Grace said as she poured a cup of coffee.

Charlotte studied her sister. Grace appeared weary, and she had shadows under her eyes.

Grace retrieved the milk from the fridge. “I didn’t tell you, did I?” She paused while stirring milk into her coffee.

“Tell me what?” Charlotte unwrapped a stick of soft butter and dropped it into the bowl.

“Luke’s watch is missing.”

Charlotte froze. “Wait. What?”

Grace leaned against the counter. She took a sip of the brew, then filled her sister in. “I’ve been racking my brain all night about where his watch could be. Would you help me search the public rooms later?”

“Of course,” Charlotte said. “Maybe he just misplaced it. I’ve done that tons of times." She reached for an egg, then stopped. "Julep's necklace."

"I know." Grace's expression was rueful. "Two valuable items missing in one day."

Winston trotted into the room, holding a crumpled ball of paper in his mouth. He dropped it at Grace's feet and backed up slightly, watching.

"Have you been getting into the trash again? I've warned you about that." She reached down and picked up the ball.

"Maybe he wants you to throw it," Charlotte suggested. Winston did enjoy a good game of fetch now and then.

"Probably," Grace said as she unfolded the paper. "Anyway, I'm worried." She scanned the page and gasped.

Charlotte cracked another egg into the bowl. "What is it?"

"Look at this." Grace waved the paper.

When Charlotte took it, she could tell by its weight and texture that it was the inn's stationery. A second sheet, without the inn logo imprinted on the top.

"'I'm so sorry,'" Charlotte read. "'I pray you can forgive—'" That was it. The words cut off abruptly, the ink trailing away. By the feminine roundness to the lettering, Charlotte guessed a woman had written it. The only two women in residence right now were Daria and Karen. And the trash had definitely been emptied before they'd checked in.

"I wonder what this is about," Charlotte said, shaking her head. "I don't get it." *I'm so sorry . . . forgive . . .*

Grace took the sheet of paper and crumpled it up again. "Not our business, right?" She wagged a finger at Winston. "Stay out of the trash."

"Unless it was meant for Luke," Charlotte said, half-joking. What if someone *had* stolen Luke's watch? They'd been fortunate so far, but such incidents frequently happened anywhere the public gathered. From her time as head chef, she knew thieves and other wrongdoers didn't come with warning labels.

Her sister sent her a stern look. "Please don't say that. We'll figure it out."

"Sorry. That was flippant of me." Charlotte gave Grace an apologetic smile before switching on the mixer. She needed to get a move on, or breakfast would be late.

Grace and Charlotte were putting away the breakfast leftovers in the kitchen when Spencer knocked on the back door.

Charlotte happened to be closer, so she went to let him in.

"Good morning and good news," Spencer said, lugging in a metal toolbox. "The part has arrived."

Charlotte clapped. "That is *great* news. Want a cup of coffee and a piece of coffee cake to fortify yourself before you start?" Feeding Spencer was the least they could do. She knew from prior experience that he wouldn't even charge them for the repair.

Spencer set the toolbox carefully on the floor. "You had me at coffee cake," he said with a grin. "I'd love some."

Another car drove into the parking area, catching Charlotte's eye. "I guess the word's out about the coffee cake. Here comes Dean." She waited by the door to greet him while Spencer went ahead to the kitchen. She heard Grace's exclamation of relief that repairs would soon be underway.

Instead of allowing Dean to reach the door and knock, Charlotte stepped outside. "Hello, stranger," she called. "What brings you out this way?"

In response, he shook his head, lips pressed tight.

Charlotte knew that something was wrong. He wasn't walking with his usual shoulders-back confidence as he crunched across the gravel.

"Come on in," Charlotte said, holding the door open. "I've got coffee cake." She was glad to note that her teasing tone sparked a little smile.

"Sorry," Dean said as they walked down the hall to the kitchen. "I'm having a bad day."

Probably to do with Julep's necklace, she guessed. But she didn't probe, figuring he'd tell her in his own good time.

In the kitchen, Spencer was still talking to Grace about the repair, but he broke off to greet Dean. "I really enjoyed last night. The music and the food both. Great place you have there."

"Thanks," Dean said.

Grace obviously noticed his morose tone because she glanced at her sister.

Charlotte shrugged, then bustled around, pouring mugs of coffee and slicing healthy hunks of coffee cake. She handed the mugs and plates to Dean and Spencer.

Dean finished the cake in several bites and set the plate on the counter. "Good stuff." He took a sip of coffee, then cleared his throat. "We didn't find Julep's necklace."

Although Charlotte had suspected as much, the shock of his words still gave her a jolt. She'd been hoping that the necklace would turn up somewhere in the inn. This was really bad news.

Before she could comment, Dean went on. "As you know, Charlotte, we searched last night without any luck. So this morning in the light of day, we scoured the place. We even emptied the trash cans and pawed through the garbage."

An unhappy silence fell over the kitchen.

"Do you think someone stole it?" Spencer asked, his voice somber.

"That's the only option left," Dean answered. "But I hate to think one of my staff . . . We have a good team, and I run background checks before I hire."

Spencer, who used to be an intelligence analyst for the FBI, put his mug down and straightened his shoulders. "Hold on. Let's take a step back. Do you have proof Julep was wearing the necklace?" His voice was crisp, authoritative.

A crease appeared between Grace's brows. "I don't remember seeing it, but Julep claimed she was. And she's sharp as a tack, so I believe her."

"The chamber had someone taking photos last night. Let's find out if Julep is in any of them." Dean removed his phone from his pocket and brought up the chamber site. He placed his phone on the counter so they could all see it. After scrolling through several shots, he gave a grunt of satisfaction. "There she is."

Julep was standing by her table talking to a small group. A glittering necklace was clearly visible above the scoop-necked blouse she wore with a jacket.

"So now we know that she was wearing it." Spencer pointed at the faces in the photograph. "I know Atticus and Luke. Who are the other people?"

While Grace and Dean named everyone, Charlotte studied Luke. He stood nearby, appearing to listen. Or was he actually scoping out Julep's necklace?

A shiver of revulsion rippled through Charlotte. Oh, how she detested to suspect people, especially a guest she liked. But she couldn't help but wonder if Luke's watch had really been stolen. Or was it merely a fabrication to distract from a larger crime?

She glanced at Grace, who returned her gaze. Without her sister saying a word, Charlotte knew she shared her concerns about the young astronomy professor.

Spencer sighed. "I'm sorry to say this, Dean, since it reflects on your business, but Julep should file a police report. She'll need one for the insurance claim."

Dean set his jaw. "You're absolutely right. I'll call her right away." He drained his coffee and returned the mug to the counter, then tucked his phone into his pocket. "Thanks for the coffee break, ladies. I'd better get on it."

As he strode out of the kitchen, Charlotte noticed again the dejected set of his shoulders. She hated to see the confident, good-natured Dean so disheartened. It wasn't natural.

"Maybe we should ask Luke to file one too," Charlotte told Grace. His reaction to that suggestion might be telling. Frankly, Charlotte hoped it cleared him.

"File a police report?" Spencer asked. "Why? Is something else missing?"

Grace nodded. "Luke lost his watch yesterday. He thought he left it in his room, but we're going to check the rest of the inn, just in case."

"Is it valuable?" Spencer asked.

"I think so," Grace replied. "He said it's an heirloom, so it's probably an antique."

"Not one of those drugstore watches, then." Spencer gritted his teeth. "I hope we don't have a pro jewel thief in town."

A professional jewel thief? If she considered thefts at all, Charlotte regarded many of them as crimes of opportunity. Snatching a purse. Rummaging through unlocked cars. Calling the perpetrator a professional added a layer of planning and forethought that was downright chilling. Even break-ins targeting electronics and cash weren't on that level. Most of the time.

"Why would that type of thief come to Magnolia Harbor?" Grace asked, distress sharpening her usually soft voice. "It's not like we're millionaires around here."

Spencer put up a hand. "I'm sorry. I may be jumping the gun." He attempted a smile. "Sometimes I forget I'm not on the job anymore. We were paid to be suspicious and try to make connections between crimes."

Grace bit her lower lip. "What can we do? This is a terrible situation. Our guests' valuables and the inn's reputation are at stake."

Charlotte's heart sank at the truth of her sister's words. They'd spent years cultivating an impeccable standing in the lodging industry. Could they lose it all in an instant? The fact that other inns and hotels commonly suffered from thefts was little comfort at the moment. And poor Dean. He was in the same boat.

Spencer winced. "Now I really feel bad. Please don't panic yet. Look for that watch again. Hopefully, it will turn up soon. And remind your guests to be careful, to lock valuables in the inn safe, etc."

"Good idea. If they do that, then they should be fine." Grace wiped her hands across her apron with resolution. "Charlotte, let's go search for Luke's watch. With any luck, we'll find it."

Two hours later, they still hadn't located the watch, despite practically tearing apart the first-floor rooms.

With a sigh of frustration, Charlotte sank into a sofa in the living room. "I don't think it's down here."

Winnie, who'd been helping, threw up her hands. "I agree. I even checked inside all the vases and went through the magazine racks. We really need to thin those out, by the way."

"Feel free to recycle them." Grace nibbled on a finger. "Frankly, I'm stumped. I can't think of anywhere else to look."

"Maybe Luke will find it," Winnie said. She folded her hands. "I'm praying that he will."

Partway through their quest, he'd wandered through the inn, and Grace had asked him to check his room again.

A stream of cool air began to flow through the vents above

Charlotte's head, and she leaned back, placing herself in the direct line of fire. "At least the AC is fixed."

"It's such a relief," Grace said.

Charlotte closed her eyes for a moment. Then a thought made them pop open. "Since we're at a dead end, I'm going to go make ice cream." She pushed herself to her feet. "Today calls for chocolate. And lots of it."

Karen

"Winnie, look at this." Holding the painting by the edges, Karen hurried down the last couple of stairs. She stopped in front of the reception desk and held up the imitation van Gogh for the older woman to see.

"You finished that already?" Winnie's mouth fell open. "But I just gave it to you yesterday."

Karen set the painting down on the desktop. "I know." She laughed. "I was up almost all night." She studied the whorls and swirls, remembering how she had dabbed each little section of color. A cool breeze hit her back where she was standing, and she glanced up. "The AC is back on."

"It sure is." Winnie fanned herself with a brochure, bringing the cooler air her way. "And I am so grateful."

"Me too," Karen said. She traced a finger along the edge of the painting. "I'm trying to decide what to do next."

"What do you mean?"

"Another project."

Winnie nodded toward the music room. "There are other kits in there, I think. Help yourself."

Karen considered doing that, but it didn't feel quite right. A tiny idea dawned in her mind, exactly as if a light were shining through a cracked door. Could she? Should she? Yes. Certainty flooded her as the door opened wide. "I'd like to buy some art supplies. Is there a place in town?"

Karen got off the shuttle in historic downtown Magnolia Harbor. She'd decided not to drive since Winnie said parking could be a problem. Judging by the number of people in town, she was right.

After waiting at the crosswalk with a group, Karen headed for The Book Cottage. Main Street was an enchanting, tree-shaded enclave of cobblestone streets and charming vintage storefronts. The atmosphere was slow-paced yet festive, and Karen found herself relaxing as she strolled. That was the name for a feeling of lightness and tranquility, right? She'd almost forgotten.

Karen spotted the bookstore down the block, but she took her time getting there, pausing to window-shop along the way. Miss Millie's had the cutest summer dresses in the window. Maybe she'd splurge and buy one. The concerts were a good excuse, since people dressed up for those.

A trickle of unease ran down her spine as she remembered the events of last night. Hopefully, they had found Julep's necklace. Being accused of stealing it had not been pleasant, to say the least. She shrugged off the memory, resolving not to blame Magnolia Harbor for one woman's misplaced suspicion.

Inside the bookstore, the familiar scents of fresh paper and ink greeted her. The place was bustling, with people browsing in the various sections.

A woman with a highlighted brown bob sat behind the counter. She glanced up at Karen with a smile. "Welcome to The Book Cottage."

"Can you tell me where the art supplies are?" Karen asked as she approached the counter. A flash of uncertainty made her words waver. Who was she to call herself an artist? She hadn't lifted a paintbrush in years. Then a rush of warmth flowed over her. Yes, she had, last night with dear Vincent's masterpiece.

She must have been grinning because the woman's smile grew even wider. She pointed to the back corner of the store. "Over there. Let me know if you need help." She patted the name badge pinned to her chest. "I'm Blanche, the owner."

"Nice to meet you. I'm Karen. I'm staying at the Magnolia Harbor Inn."

Blanche nodded. "Grace and Charlotte are good folks. I'm sure they're treating you right."

"They certainly are." Karen thanked Blanche and headed toward the art supplies. Along the way, brightly colored book jackets called out to her, but she ignored them. Maybe she'd return and browse another time. Right now, she had a mission, and if she got distracted, she might lose her motivation again. Inspiration was precious, and in her case, it had to be coddled like a fragile egg that otherwise wouldn't hatch.

Smiling at her analogy, Karen reached the art section. She stopped to take it in and orient herself. For such a small store, the inventory was quite extensive. There were racks of canvases, boxes of paint tubes, both oil and watercolor, sketch pads, pencils, and charcoal. She could spend lots of money in here.

After a few minutes of deliberation, Karen selected a sketch pad, pencils, a watercolor set, paper, and brushes. She wasn't staying long enough to paint something in oils, which could take ages to dry. She stacked the items in her arms and juggled them over to the counter, relieved not to drop anything.

Blanche didn't bat an eye when Karen dumped it all onto the counter. "Did you find everything you need?" She grabbed a pencil before it could roll off.

"I think so," Karen said. She took a deep breath. "I'm just getting back into painting again. Starting off slow." There. She'd said it aloud—again. She was a painter. And each time she felt a little more solid in her assertion.

"We get many artists here," Blanche said, scanning the first item. She set it gently into a shopping bag propped by a frame. "Magnolia Harbor has some beautiful scenery to paint."

"It sure does," Karen agreed. Glancing around the store, she saw a familiar woman walking toward the checkout, long blonde hair swinging.

Daria's footsteps hitched, eyes widening in recognition. "Hi, Karen. Buying books?" She held several in her hands.

"No, art supplies." Karen gestured toward her items. "But I'll probably be back later for books. There's a great selection."

Blanche smiled in acknowledgment and kept scanning.

"I'll say." Daria stood with her hip cocked, the books cradled in her arms. "Want to get lunch with me? I hear there's a great Thai place down the street."

"Why Thai," Blanche said. "It's very good." She reached under the counter and pulled out two coupons. "Good for 20 percent off."

Karen picked up a coupon. "Now we have to go." She and Daria laughed.

After Daria checked out, the pair made their way down the street, Book Cottage bags swinging from their hands. They passed Miss Millie's.

"I'm going to buy a dress," Karen announced, stopping on the sidewalk. "What do you think of the pale-green one?"

Daria cocked her head, studying the plain linen dress with its fitted bodice and slender skirt. "I think it will look fabulous with your coloring." She regarded Karen's face. "Wow. I've never seen greenish-gold eyes like yours before."

"Yeah, that's what they tell me," Karen said, pretending to shrug off the compliment but secretly enjoying it. Shifting the conversation away from herself, she said, "You'd look great in that." The periwinkle-blue dress had a vintage vibe, with a full skirt and thin straps. A band of the same color appliquéd daisies marched around the hem.

"Oh, I love it." Daria took Karen's arm. "Let's go try them on before we eat lunch."

Karen reached for the door handle. "After you."

Half an hour later, they were seated outside Why Thai, bags from Miss Millie's nestled next to the bookstore purchases. Big white bowls filled with fragrant curry sat in front of them. Karen had chosen Massaman curry with beef and potatoes, and Daria was eating Phanaeng Panang curry with shrimp.

Daria dug in, using a ceramic spoon to scoop up rice, vegetables, and shrimp. "This is so good."

"I love curry." Karen took a moment to savor the mingled flavors. "I ate lots of rice dishes in Africa, but they had a totally different taste." She thought back to Jollof rice, which featured tomatoes and hot peppers and sweet and savory spices and herbs.

"Stews and soups are comforting, aren't they?" Daria said. "My grammy used to make doodle soup. It's a Tennessee delicacy."

"Is that where you grew up?"

Daria nodded.

"So, what's in doodle soup?" Karen asked. Weren't there such a thing as doodlebugs? But surely no one ate them. Although in Africa, some people considered grasshoppers a delicacy.

"I know what you're thinking. I've gotten that look before." In between bites, Daria explained the simple recipe. "Broth from your roasted meat of choice. We usually used chicken. Then add vinegar, salt, and cayenne pepper, either ground or whole. A little flour to thicken the broth. And that's it."

Karen tried to imagine the soup's flavor, especially the vinegar. "It's interesting how almost every cuisine uses peppers. I've heard they're good for you."

Daria laughed. "That's my theory, and I'm sticking to it. I love spicy food." She went on, mentioning memorable meals and dishes from around the country.

"Wow, you've been everywhere," Karen said. "Although I worked in Africa, I've never been to the West Coast of the United States or even the Midwest."

"Well, that's the price of a singing career," Daria said lightly. "We go where the work is." A shadow drifted through her big blue eyes. "Sometimes I do miss home." She swallowed. "And family. What there is of it."

Karen's heart went out to the young singer. From her expression and the pain in her words, Karen guessed that she was no stranger to hardship. "Do you see your grammy very often?"

Daria shook her head. "Grammy's gone. I only have a sister. Oh, and Darryl, of course." Her gaze was distant. "My sister was badly hurt in an accident."

"Oh no." Karen put a hand to her chest, thinking of her own sister. "Is she okay?"

"Not quite. But getting better." Again, Daria didn't look directly at Karen when she said this.

Karen took another scoop of curry. "Well, I hope she heals up nicely." She sensed the subject held great pain for Daria, so she scoured her mind for another topic. "Guess what? I'm going fishing later."

The conversation turned to humorous fishing trips as they finished their lunch.

Daria checked the time. "I should return to the inn. I need to rest before tonight's performance."

"I'll go with you," Karen offered.

After collecting their bags, the pair walked through town toward the shuttle stop.

"We'll definitely have to come back downtown," Daria said to Karen. "I haven't been shopping with a friend for a while. It was fun." Her smile appeared genuine, all troubling thoughts apparently gone.

"I enjoyed it too," Karen said. "I'm wearing my new dress tonight." They paused at the crosswalk near the park. "Oh, good. They have an officer directing traffic."

The police officer, who was thickset and muscular and sported a buzz cut, was stopping cars to let groups of pedestrians cross the street at intervals.

Daria moved aside, seemingly to let another person by, but as they crossed the street, Karen noticed she stayed to her left, almost hovering in Karen's shadow. But once they reached the other side, Daria moved ahead. It was obvious enough for Karen to notice. She glanced over her shoulder at the cop. He was watching them, his eyes hidden behind sunglasses.

A few minutes later, the shuttle pulled up and stopped with a hiss of brakes.

As they were getting ready to board, Daria put a hand on Karen's arm. "I'm not going back on this shuttle. But I'll see you at the inn later."

"Okay. Have a good afternoon." Puzzled, Karen got into the van. Didn't Daria say she wanted to rest? But as the shuttle pulled away from the curb, she saw Daria strolling across the grass toward the lake.

Karen reminded herself that it wasn't her business. With a shrug, she turned her thoughts to the fishing expedition. She'd need to bring plenty of sunscreen and wear a hat.

"Hello, gentlemen," Karen greeted as she set her tote down on the grass beside the dock.

Luke, Osgood, and a tall, thin man were puttering around a motorboat in preparation for the fishing trip.

"Karen, I'm glad you could join us." Luke's grin was genuine. He introduced her to Pete, the only man she didn't know.

Pete, who had a long, morose face and wore wire-rimmed spectacles, gave her a brief smile and a wave.

"Thanks for letting me tag along. I haven't been fishing in ages." Karen flashed on a memory of boats venturing out onto an African lake. "What are we catching today?"

"Big cats," Pete said, his voice as laconic as his appearance. With a smirk, he clarified, "Otherwise known as catfish."

A Southern delicacy, excellent breaded and fried. "They have those in Africa too," Karen said. "Including electric catfish."

Luke whistled. "I've heard of those. They can emit up to 350 volts."

"Nothing like that here," Osgood said. "Only good eating. You hear about the hundred-pounder a woman caught on Lake Moultrie?"

Karen tried to imagine such an enormous beast. It would take up most of the open space in the boat.

Luke handed her a life jacket, which she put on. Then he helped her into the boat. She walked to the middle, careful not to step on any of the fishing gear, and sat down on a bench.

The men clambered aboard. With Osgood at the helm, they buzzed out into the lake. The outboard motor was quite noisy, so Karen contented herself with gazing at the view while the men discussed, with many gestures and pointing, where to go.

Peace had surrounded her all day like a mantle. Until her thoughts took a turn they shouldn't. Maybe it was the way the pale sun glowed through the haze. Or the relentless sound of water lapping against the hull.

Karen was back in her tent, unable to get off her cot. She was racked with chills, burning with heat. And the dreams . . . they were more like nightmares. She had trouble discerning between what was real and what was the product of a feverish brain.

Luke scooted onto the bench. "Are you okay?" he asked, leaning close.

Karen turned, her tongue mute. She couldn't see his eyes behind the sunglasses.

As if realizing that, he lifted them, his brown eyes squinting against the glare.

She nodded. "Sorry. It happens sometimes." Her voice sounded hoarse. She patted her chest. "Water?"

"Of course." Luke rummaged through a cooler, removed a bottle of water, and twisted off the cap. Then he handed her the bottle.

"Thanks." Karen drained it, wishing the cold water could wash away her memories. She held out the empty bottle, not sure what to do with it.

Luke took it and tucked it back into the cooler, along with the cap. Then he raised his chin and sat facing forward, the breeze ruffling his hair.

The interruption had helped. Karen was able to focus on her surroundings again, study the houses on the shore and on a nearby island. She held on with a laugh when a larger boat's wake made their craft rock from side to side.

Osgood headed toward a cove shaded by huge trees. Here the water was dark and still. The motor cut and they drifted.

"See the freshwater mussels floating on the surface?" Osgood pointed overboard. "Catfish love those."

Pete rubbed his hands together. "We're coming for you."

The men set up the fishing poles, which they placed in racks at the back of the boat. Once the fish took the bait, they'd pick up the poles and reel them in. Then they settled in to wait.

Karen was prepared for this. She reached into her bag and pulled out a sketch pad and charcoal. The tree branches arching over the water not only looked beautiful, but the scene *felt* right in her creative brain. With a sigh of relief, Karen began to sketch. Her artistic vision wasn't gone. It had only been in hiding.

"Here we go!" Pete shouted.

Karen whirled around to see a definite tug on one line. The reel began to whir. Then another line activated. And a third.

"Get that one, will you?" Luke yelled to Karen.

To her surprise, she saw they'd set up four lines. She put her pad and charcoal aside and jumped up. "What do I do?"

Luke gave directions to her in between taking care of his own line.

Pete's line snapped, the reel spinning uselessly. "Oh no, there he goes."

Osgood grunted. "I've got one. Come on." He managed to bring up a good-size fish.

Pete netted it, then announced, "Twenty-seven inches at least."

Luke brought his fish to the surface. It wasn't one they wanted, so he cut it free.

Now all eyes were on Karen, still fighting to bring the creature in.

"Please help me, someone," she called. "I can't hang on much longer." The pole was bent in an arc, the line almost played out. She couldn't believe the fish hadn't snapped the line already.

The fish rose to the surface, thrashing and spinning.

She braced her feet against the bottom of the boat, every muscle in her back and arms straining. Was it possible he would pull her into the water?

Luke helped her hang on to the rod while Osgood got the net ready.

When the silvery fish came up out of the water, Pete whistled. "That one makes yours look puny, Osgood."

"It's about forty pounds," Luke said. He had to help the older man navigate it into the boat.

Karen stared at the huge fish in disbelief. It had to be three feet long. "What on earth are we going to do with that?"

Luke's teeth shone white against his tan. "Catfish fry coming right up."

"Sounds good," Karen said with a laugh. "Just don't make me clean it."

The others laughed too.

Shaking the tiredness out of her limbs, Karen lifted her face to the sun. The mantle of peace fell around her again.

She hoped it would stay this time.

14

Daria

Daria knew she should return to the inn for rehearsal. Darryl was going to be furious if she was late. But somehow she couldn't make herself get off the bench. She closed her eyes, allowing the sounds of a breeze rustling the oak leaves and the ruffle of gentle waves against the shore to wash over her.

She had enjoyed shopping and lunch with Karen so much. But now she felt empty and forlorn, her profound loneliness underscored by the sharing and laughter. In a few days, she and Karen would go their separate ways and never see each other again. Daria and Darryl never stayed in one place long enough for her to make friends.

It didn't matter anyway. Daria imagined the horror on Karen's face if she knew the truth. The disgust and rejection that would surely follow. As they should.

Daria was a criminal. She didn't deserve friends or love or a home. A sob forced its way up past her ribs.

"Miss, are you all right?" The policeman who had been directing traffic stood in front of her, hands on his hips. He lifted his sunglasses briefly, revealing concerned blue eyes.

Daria swiped at her eyes, her vision blurry with tears. Did he know who she was? Had he come to question her about last night? She'd gone cold with terror when Julep had raised the alarm about her necklace. And then poor Karen had been accused of theft. It had been all she could do to hold her tongue.

Darryl had done it, of course. On the way back to the inn, he'd gloated about how he'd covertly lifted the necklace without the older woman noticing. He'd even flexed his fingers, boasting of his light touch on more than the piano keys.

After Daria had finally reached the privacy of her room, she'd thrown up, sickened by Darryl, sickened by her life.

Now, staring at the policeman while blinking away tears, urgent words crowded to her lips, begging to be spoken. She could end everything right now, stop the torture, blow up the false life she was leading.

Alexis. A cold wave of fear jolted her. She couldn't risk anything happening to her sister. Once she knew Alexis was okay, she would go to the police and confess. She promised.

"I'm okay," she said to the officer, trying to inject sincerity into her tone. "Thinking about someone I've lost." And that was the truth.

He studied her face for a long moment. "I wanted to make sure no one had been bothering you."

"No, I haven't talked to a soul." Daria made herself smile. "I've been sitting here all by my lonesome." She allowed a little Southern accent to creep into her voice.

The officer didn't appear convinced. Maybe he thought she was having a breakdown. And maybe he was right. "If you need any help, someone to talk to, maybe, we're only a phone call away."

Daria lifted a hand. "Good to know. I appreciate you checking on me." She forced another smile. "I'm just enjoying the shade. It's hot as blazes." She fanned her face with her hand.

The officer glanced at the sky, which was white with haze. "It sure is a scorcher. Well, you take care, ma'am." After adjusting his hat, he turned and ambled off.

Daria studied his back until he was out of sight, her head spinning with relief. She slumped against the bench. She'd gotten away with it this time.

But how much longer could she keep up the charade?

From the very first note Daria sang at the impressive Jackson House Museum, she knew it wouldn't be her best performance. To perform at her best, her mind, body, and soul needed to be in harmony, work together as one. Her singing this evening could be characterized as stumbling down a sidewalk on the wrong foot.

She closed her eyes briefly against the brilliant glow from a crystal chandelier, hoping to use the interlude between songs to compose herself.

As Darryl's fingers rippled over the introductory notes of her last song, he sent her a covert look of warning. He'd noticed her sloppiness, the fact that she hadn't quite achieved that top note.

Daria glanced away. She focused on the wall straight ahead, her gaze above the rows of elegantly dressed listeners, and inhaled deeply. When she opened her mouth, she sounded much more in control. Good. At least she could end the concert well. She hoped that was all the patrons would remember.

Applause was thunderous, echoing from the high ceilings.

Daria bowed, her muscles unclenching with relief. She had finished yet another performance.

Darryl took her hand when he joined her for a bow, squeezing a little too tightly. That was his reprimand. He observed every single flaw in her singing, and she knew that tomorrow's rehearsal would be relentless.

But it wasn't that she couldn't sing or had forgotten how. The soul of her music was gone. And quite simply, the lack of it could not be disguised with technique and polish.

He finally let go.

She rubbed her fingers and glared at him.

Around them rose a thunder of voices as the audience members rose from their seats. Tonight Daria and Darryl had been the final act, and next on the agenda was a buffet supper in the grand hall. The crowd gradually filed out in that direction.

Daria couldn't eat a bite. She only wanted to go back to the inn and sleep.

Darryl moved closer, and under the pretext of kissing her cheek, he whispered, "Be real nice to Atticus and his son."

She knew what that meant. In the audience were several wealthy businessmen, sleek in their evening wear, gold watches glinting on their wrists, and she was to keep them distracted with her charm.

But Daria didn't respond to Darryl's instructions. Instead, she looked around and said, "I really could use a glass of water."

"In a minute," Darryl said.

Julep appeared at her elbow. "That was magnificent, dear. Come with me. There are some people I'd like you to meet."

Conscious of Darryl watching her as she walked away, Daria gave a girlish giggle. "I hope they include that handsome man standing next to Atticus." She noticed that he had come alone and he didn't wear a wedding band. Dying inside at her deceptiveness, she whispered in Julep's ear, "Is he single?"

Julep's eyes twinkled with mischief. "He sure is, sugar. And I know he's dying to meet you too."

For a moment, as they approached the knot of men, Daria wished she was interested in one of them. If only she could fall in love and get married. That would take her away from Darryl for good. But then she glanced over her shoulder at her brother and saw the shrewd greed twisting his features. Despair swept over her in a cold wave. She'd never be free of him. Not as long as she lived.

"Abbott, I'd like you to meet someone," Julep said to Atticus's son.

As Julep made the introductions, Daria forced herself to smile and appear charming. Thankfully, she had so much practice the gracious wordplay came automatically.

Abbott Forbes was a banker in Charleston and owned one of the coveted town houses. Now that sparked unforced admiration. She allowed him to tell her all about the restorations—in meticulous detail—as he squired her out to the buffet.

While living on the road, Daria had watched her share of home improvement shows, and she favored the ones that featured historic homes. Like the Victorian mansion they were in right now. The Jackson House itself would be her next topic of conversation.

As Daria and Abbott strolled down the wide hallway, she sensed Darryl approaching, the way one might notice a shark's fin. He moved slowly but relentlessly, fixed on his target, which was Abbott. Daria's job was to keep Abbott's eyes on her, and so far, that had been incredibly easy. Guilt panged. The poor man appeared enamored.

Daria tugged Abbott to one side, allowing others to pass by. "Something's wrong with my shoe," she said. She used his arm as a support when she lifted her foot, pretending to adjust the strap of her sandal. Out of the corner of her eye, she saw Darryl moving closer, his shoes silent on the runner. "I love these shoes." She twisted her foot around for Abbott's admiration. "But the strap always hurts my ankle."

Darryl was right behind them, his hand moving stealthily toward Abbott's back pocket. If the banker turned, he would be face-to-face with her brother. Daria needed to distract their mark for another thirty seconds or so—

Daria lost her balance and tumbled sideways, forcing Abbott to grab her to keep her upright.

Abbott also noticed Darryl, and a frown creased his brow. "What are you doing?"

Darryl stepped back, smoothing his hair with one hand. "I saw Daria was about to fall over." He laughed. "Thought I'd help you rescue her."

A series of expressions flitted over Abbott's face. "I have it under control." He turned to Daria and held out his arm. "Are you all right, my dear? Let's get something to eat."

Daria smiled at him. "Yes, let's go. I'm starving." She wasn't hungry, but what was one more lie on the heap? Somehow she had to cover their blunder so Abbott would lose the suspicion in his eyes. As for Darryl, she knew that punishment was certain. Maybe he'd cool down by the time they left.

No such luck. The chilly atmosphere during the ride back to the inn told Daria that Darryl hadn't forgiven or forgotten the incident. She shrank against the passenger door, tempted to bring it up and get it all over with. Let him yell and rant. There was always tomorrow, right? Another opportunity to steal from blind, good-hearted people.

She pressed her hot cheek to the cool glass. Abbott had asked to take her on a date. And God help her, she wanted to go. Yes, he was older, and at first glance a bit of a stuffed shirt. The type Darryl loved to make fun of as being pompous and self-satisfied. But Abbott wasn't really like that. Daria had glimpsed something sweet in him. He'd keep her safe. A sob racked her body, and it took all she had to suppress it.

Darryl's glance was like a dagger. "You should cry. You blew it big-time." He paused, waiting for her to say something. When she remained silent, he said, "I might have been caught tonight with my hand in the cookie jar. But don't worry. If it does happen, I won't go down alone."

There was the rub. She'd gladly turn him into the police, but she'd go to jail too, and frankly she was too much of a coward to face it. Instead, she kept hoping that the ordeal would be over and she could go on with her life and put it all behind her.

Darryl turned into the lot at the inn and parked. "This isn't over. Stop by my room." He got out of the car and stalked away, leaving her to stumble along in the dark alone.

Halfway to the veranda, she stopped, caught by the beauty of the stars overhead. The humid haze had cleared tonight, pushed out by a rush of cooler air from the north.

Daria stood there for a long moment. The contrast between the sky's serene, timeless beauty and her own terrible situation struck her. If only she could soar up into the sky like a bird and fly far, far from here.

Gripped by pure despair, she whispered, "Please help me."

Somehow fortified by this simple, heartfelt prayer, she went inside. The foyer was silent, only one light burning to welcome latecomers. She climbed the stairs slowly, dreading the scene in Darryl's room. At least he wouldn't yell, not in this hushed atmosphere where a shout would be as disturbing as a gunshot.

Darryl opened the door wide at her timid knock. "Took you long enough." His voice was a low growl but no less menacing than a full roar. He marched away, unfastening one of his cuff links.

Daria shut the door softly behind her, watching him much like a bird would watch a cat. She decided to let him bring it up. Why should she do it?

Darryl unfastened the other cuff link, then set the pair on the bureau.

She noticed a gold watch on the bureau. It was a familiar watch, since she was trained to notice such details. Without thinking, she dashed over and snatched it up. "Where did you get this?" She shook it at him. "It belongs to Luke."

Darryl sneered. "Aren't you observant? The fool left his door ajar.

So it was in and out lickety-split."

She shook the watch again. "But we don't steal where we're staying. That was a totally stupid move."

He was in her face in a flash. "Your little maneuver tonight was too. What were you doing? Trying to help your new boyfriend?" Malice dripped from his words.

So Darryl had noticed Abbott's attentiveness and her favorable response. Daria stifled a sigh. "No, it was an accident. I overbalanced. You try standing on one foot in heels."

His gaze bored into hers. "Don't let it happen again."

Dredging up courage she didn't even know she possessed, she dropped the watch onto the bureau. "Don't steal where we're staying again."

Darryl moved slightly away, arms folded across his chest. "Nope. I'm afraid I can't meet that condition. Our biggest heist is happening right here in a few days."

Daria's knees went weak, and she sank into the closest chair. This was dreadful. She'd been hoping that he would choose a different location. She couldn't steal from Grace, Charlotte, and Winnie. The theft of Luke's watch was bad enough. "What's the plan?" she asked, her voice trembling.

He shook his head. "Tell you so you can blow it? I don't think so."

How could she stop him if she didn't know what he was planning to do? All of it—the fear, the deception, the cruelty of stealing from would-be friends, the sense of being trapped—tangled like a huge web of pain and guilt in Daria's midsection.

Without even thinking about it, she launched herself from the chair and ran for the house phone. Her cell phone was in her room. She picked up the receiver and began to dial.

"What are you doing?" Darryl tried to wrest the receiver away from her, attempting to hit the button to disconnect.

Daria blocked him with her body, then stomped on his bare foot with her heel.

He cried out in pain and hopped away.

"This has gone on long enough," she said. "I'm calling Alexis, and then I'm getting out of here."

Instead of attacking her again, Darryl laughed.

His response was so unexpected that she stopped punching numbers and stared at him.

"You can call her, but it won't do any good."

Cold dread washed over Daria. "What do you mean?" Her voice was a harsh whisper.

Darryl hobbled closer, pointing a finger at her. "Alexis is dead. I wasn't going to tell you—"

She didn't wait to hear the rest. She slammed the receiver down. Shaking, stunned with shock, she hugged herself. "Then it doesn't matter anymore. I'm going to the police."

"Go ahead, my darling little sister, and I'll give them that." He motioned to Luke's watch. "With your fingerprints all over it."

Daria ran blindly for the door. Alexis was dead, and it was all her fault.

Grace

Grace studied the long to-do list with dismay. "How are we going to get all this done before tomorrow night?" She pushed a hand through her hair, already disheveled due to a previous review of the formidable set of tasks.

The inn was hosting the capstone performance of the series, featuring accomplished musicians from around the country. More than a hundred people were expected to attend.

That was all fine, but they'd just gotten word that a Charleston lifestyle magazine was going to feature the event and the inn. "We'll also include recipes," the editor had said. "The writer and photographer will arrive tomorrow afternoon." The opportunity was too good to pass up, but it meant taking the preparations up a notch.

Charlotte filled Grace's cup with fresh coffee. "Hang in there. We've got Helping Hands Cleaning coming in, and Edible Delights Catering is working with me on food prep."

Grace cocked a brow. "You're awfully calm about this. They want recipes and food photographs, remember?" She picked up the mug and took a sip, despite not being sure if all the caffeine was helping or hindering.

Charlotte set the carafe back in its place. "I'm viewing it as an opportunity to promote the inn and build buzz about my new cookbook." She opened a drawer, pulled out a glossy flyer, and gave it to her sister. "Look at this mock-up I put together. I'm going to set it on a stand on the table."

Grace studied the flyer. A photograph of strawberry shortcake from an earlier event that summer formed the background. "'*Comfort and Cheer from Magnolia Harbor Inn*, a cookbook featuring the inn's best recipes,'" she read out loud.

"Do you like it?" Charlotte asked.

"Yes, it looks good," Grace said, placing the flyer on the counter. In her former life at a marketing firm, she'd often created materials for clients. Charlotte was showing quite a talent for design.

Charlotte beamed. "I copied the layout from one of your old ads."

Grace laughed. "So what's on the menu?"

"I'm thinking we'll do an ice cream buffet tomorrow night. That will make a great photo opportunity, and I'll give the magazine a couple of the recipes. Since Edible Delights will be doing the main dishes and appetizers, I can concentrate on making ice cream."

"Sounds great. What kind of flavors are you going to make?"

Charlotte flew over to the other counter, picked up a piece of paper, and handed it to Grace. "What do you think?"

Grace scanned the selections—vanilla bean, espresso granita, toasted coconut, Mexican chocolate, and fruit bombe. She could picture the different colors and textures displayed in a photograph. "They sound delicious. We'll need to get out the glass dishes and silver."

"Oh yeah," Charlotte said. "I was going to use cones and disposable dishes until we heard from the magazine."

"Polish the silver," Grace muttered, adding that task to the list. "Thank goodness we have a set for a hundred."

They'd bought a large set at an auction, thinking they might need it for events. Many weddings and other parties at the inn used nice disposable utensils, but the real silver had come out of storage more than once.

Winnie entered the kitchen and headed straight for the coffeepot.

"Good morning." She poured a cup. "The Helping Hands van just pulled in."

Grace's spirits lifted. "Many hands make light work, right?"

Her sister groaned at the pun.

"True in this case," Winnie said. "Why don't I supervise them while you work on something else?"

"Would you?" Grace was overcome with gratitude for her aunt. "I've got to run to the chamber of commerce and get the programs. Missy is short-staffed and can't deliver them like she'd planned." Grace was probably—no, definitely—putting off polishing the silver, but maybe the short break would help her to organize her thoughts.

Charlotte popped to the other side of the kitchen and brought Grace another piece of paper. "If you're going to town, I have this list for the grocery store." She regarded her sister with hopeful brown eyes.

Grace sighed. "I'll stop by Hanson's after I go to the chamber." With an eye on the clock, she drained her coffee. "Guess I'd better get going."

Winston barked and danced at her feet, obviously hoping to go along.

"Sorry, boy, but you need to stay here," Grace said.

Winnie tossed him a treat. "You can help me supervise the cleaners, Winston."

He gobbled up the treat, then barked and danced again, seeming satisfied by the prospect.

A rapping sounded on the back door.

"And there they are," Winnie announced.

Grace waved to Tammy Snyder and her crew as she headed to her car. The three women were unloading buckets of cleaning supplies and extra vacuum cleaners. They were so efficient and fast that they might even be done by the time Grace got back.

She glanced at the yard. The grass was really growing and could use a trim. After getting into her car, she called the lawn service to see if they could come early this week. With the magazine arriving, the inn needed to look its best.

Grace drove downtown to the chamber of commerce, located in a quaint former train station. As she walked to the door, she regarded the welcoming porch with a smile.

Missy sat behind the desk, answering visitor inquiries and inserting letters into envelopes. When Grace walked in, she smiled and nodded in acknowledgment while not missing a beat.

Knowing that she'd have to wait a few minutes, Grace sat down and leafed through a magazine.

"Where is the Magnolia Harbor Inn?" a feminine voice asked Missy.

Grace glanced up at this mention of her inn. A young woman wearing a huge straw hat and sunglasses stood at the desk. Her light-brown hair was in a bun, and she was dressed in a flowing floral skirt and peasant blouse and sandals. Rather than barge into the conversation, Grace decided to let Missy handle it.

Missy gave directions to the inn and pressed a brochure into the woman's hands. "It's one of our finest lodging options. And the food is out of this world. The chef writes cookbooks. Charlotte Wylde."

The woman studied the brochure for a moment. She thanked Missy, then turned and left, bells above the door jingling.

"Thanks for the sales pitch." Grace set aside the magazine and stood.

"I meant every word." Missy rolled her chair back and forth on casters as she rearranged things on her desk and the adjacent credenza. "I thought of introducing you, but I didn't want to put both of you on the spot."

"Good call," Grace said. "I'd hate for someone to feel pressured to make a reservation. Besides, we're full until next week."

"I love hearing that." Missy bent over and picked up a small box, which she thumped onto the desk. "Here are the programs. Thanks for coming down. My helper called in sick, so I can't leave until one of the volunteers shows up."

"I'm trying to get everything ready today," Grace said. She paused, knowing Missy would enjoy the news she was about to share. "Since a writer from *Low Country Life* is coming to the inn tomorrow."

Missy squealed and clapped. "They're featuring the inn? Why, that's fabulous."

"From what I understand, it's a feature about the inn and the musical event. We're thrilled." Grace picked up the box. "Thanks. See you tomorrow night?"

"I'll be there with bells on," the chamber director promised. With Missy's flamboyant personality and style, that wasn't much of an exaggeration.

Outside the chamber building, Grace spotted Luke strolling her way. A knot tightened in her belly. She really needed to discuss the missing watch with him. There hadn't been an opportunity to do so at breakfast.

"Want some help with that?" Luke reached out for the box. He peeked inside the open flaps. "For tomorrow night, I'm guessing?"

"Yes, they are." Grace pointed to her vehicle. "I'm parked over there." As they walked, she asked, "Doing a little shopping or sightseeing?"

"Shopping." Luke rolled his eyes with a grin. "I need to buy something for my niece and nephew. I never should have started bringing them presents from my trips. Now they expect gifts every time I go somewhere."

Grace smiled. "We have a good bookstore. They have stuff for kids."

"Thanks for the recommendation. I'll check it out." Luke shifted the box, waiting while Grace unlocked the door.

She stowed the box on the floor, an urgency to discuss the topic building. But frankly she was stalling, wishing she didn't have to ruin their day. Finally, she took a deep breath and said, "Did you file a police report?" She thought she knew the answer since she hadn't heard from the local force.

He shook his head. "Not yet. I'm giving it a couple more days. Maybe the watch will turn up."

"I hope so." Grace thought about the cleaners. Maybe they would find it. "But I'm serious. We need to take care of it before you check out. If it doesn't turn up."

Luke shrugged. "I think it will. I've been praying about it."

A rush of gladness filled Grace. Just hearing those words made her feel more hopeful. "Well, here's to answered prayers." She waved her keys. "I've got to get to the grocery store. See you back at the inn."

With a nod and a wave, he headed up the sidewalk.

As Grace watched him go, she saw how he courteously helped a young mother navigate a twin stroller across the street. She whispered a prayer that Luke's faith would be rewarded.

The parking lot at Hanson's Farm Fresh Foods was busy. Grace found a parking spot, then made sure she had her list before getting out of the car. She hated trying to shop from memory. She always forgot some vital ingredient.

On the way into the store, she spotted a familiar tall, lean figure cutting through the lot. Spencer was heading toward the entrance too. She stopped to wait. "Hey, Spencer," she said with a smile. She moved to one side to allow others to go through the doors.

"Hey, Grace," he said in return, his expression warm with greeting. "How are you today?"

"I'm fine." *Now.* Something about Spencer always made her day a little brighter. "Busy getting ready for the concert at the inn."

"Jerzy Flynn's performance." He grinned. "I bought my ticket already."

Jerzy was a renowned if eccentric mandolin player, the headliner tomorrow night.

"Yes, we're expecting a hundred people. And guess what?" Grace hesitated to build suspense. "A team from *Low Country Life* is coming. They want to feature the inn."

Spencer whistled, long and low. "That's fantastic." He brushed a hand along the front of the faded T-shirt he wore to do home and garden chores. "I guess that means I'd better dress up."

"Well, I love that shirt, but yes, I would . . ." Grace drew out the words, raising her brows. This was one reason she liked Spencer so much. He brought out her teasing side and lightened the mood.

"How's the AC holding up?" he asked, gazing at the hazy sky. "This heat isn't supposed to break until maybe tomorrow night. After thunderstorms roll in."

"The AC is great. Thanks again for fixing it." Grace shuddered to think they might have had to hold the event without it. Actually, that wouldn't have been possible, especially with the crowd they were expecting. Someone would have fainted or worse. And Charlotte's ice cream would have melted into colorful puddles.

Thinking of Charlotte's ice cream reminded Grace that her sister was waiting. She waved the list. "This has been nice, but I'd better get going."

"Me too," Spencer said. "I'm in the middle of a project but realized I didn't have anything for lunch. So here I am."

The door opened automatically, but he stood back to let her enter the store first. What a gentleman. She was so glad Spencer was in her life. He even made grocery shopping a little more enjoyable.

"Good morning." Cal Gunderson smiled in greeting when they entered. The owner of the grocery store believed in the personal touch with customers.

Spencer waved and kept going.

Grace stopped to talk to Cal. "I'm hoping you have the following items." She went over the list with him, discussing the more exotic items Charlotte wanted. He had all of it in stock and directed her to the appropriate aisles.

"You're the best," Grace said. "Charlotte told me she's going to mention you in her new cookbook." Charlotte included people who helped her in the acknowledgments. And Cal had done many special orders for her. Plus, he gave them a volume discount as a local business.

Cal put a hand to his chest as though saying, "Who me?"

Grace grinned as she grabbed a cart and headed off to shop. She needed to get to work. She had silver to polish.

16

Karen

Midmorning, Karen left her third-floor nest in search of coffee. She'd been working all morning on sketches of the view from the veranda, and her energy was flagging.

Halfway down to the first floor, the buzz of vacuums rose to her ears. She continued her descent to find Winnie wiping things down with a cloth in the foyer.

When Winnie spotted Karen, she stopped working and smiled. "Good morning. Can I help you?"

Karen craned her neck, seeing that several women were busy with vacuums in the public rooms. "I was hoping for coffee, but if you're busy cleaning . . ."

"Go ahead into the kitchen," Winnie said as she started dusting again. "Charlotte just put on a pot. And there are cookies."

Moving gingerly through the rooms, hoping she wasn't disturbing anyone, Karen reached the kitchen. Here she found Charlotte reading a recipe and cracking eggs into a huge silver bowl. She glanced up with a smile.

"Don't mind me," Karen said, pointing at the coffee.

Charlotte nodded and focused on her work.

Karen filled a big mug, added cream from a pitcher set in ice, and wrapped a couple of oatmeal raisin cookies in a napkin. They should hold her over until lunch when she planned to go downtown. She tiptoed back to the foyer.

A woman was setting a large, ornate flower arrangement on the counter. She had Winnie sign a clipboard, then left.

"Nice flowers," Karen said. In addition to roses, there were orchids and other exotic blooms she couldn't name.

Winnie checked the envelope. "They're for Daria. I think she's in her room." She frowned. "But I hate to disturb her in case she's resting."

"Why don't I take up a note? I can stick it on her door." Karen studied the flowers again, wondering who sent them. But someone of Daria's beauty and talent must often get flowers from admirers and fans.

"Good idea." Winnie rummaged behind the desk, pulled out a large pad of sticky notes, and scrawled a message. She peeled it off and handed it to Karen. "Thanks for doing that. We're trying to get ready for tomorrow night's performance."

"Aha. I saw that on the calendar. It's going to be nice, having a concert right here." Karen waved the finger holding the note. "Very convenient."

Winnie gave her directions to Daria's room, and Karen headed upstairs, careful not to slop her coffee. Outside the Dogwood Suite, she pressed the note to the door with the sticky side, hoping it would stay on.

Karen was turning away when the door opened a crack. "I hope I didn't disturb you," she said. "I tried to be quiet."

"I was awake." Daria's voice was a croak. She opened the door wider, revealing a tear-ravaged face and disheveled hair. She opened her mouth, and a deep sob erupted.

Karen froze. Now what? She barely knew Daria and had no interest in intruding upon private moments. But then her innate compassion kicked in. She set the coffee and cookies on a handy nearby table and engulfed Daria in a hug. She made shushing sounds as the woman continued to cry.

Daria wiped her eyes. "Would you like to come in?"

Karen followed her into the dim room. The curtains were closed tightly against the sunshine.

Daria plucked tissues from a box, sniffing. "I'm sorry. It's just that I got bad news last night."

Very bad news, judging by Daria's obvious distress. "I'm so sorry," Karen said. "If you want to talk, I'm here."

Daria didn't respond for a few moments. "Forgive me. I'm kind of in a daze." She gestured at the conversation grouping near the fireplace. "Please have a seat."

Karen perched on the edge of an armchair. Daria sat on the sofa, her gaze on the tissue she was destroying with her fingers.

A heavy silence fell, and again Karen wondered if she should leave the poor woman alone.

"This is so hard for me," Daria finally whispered. "I haven't told anyone." She looked at Karen in entreaty. "Can I trust you? I mean, really trust you?"

Karen's heart leaped in alarm. Daria's request told her this situation was far from simple. With the sensation that she might be stepping onto thin ice over dangerous waters, she said, "Yes, you can. Whatever you say to me stays here. I promise."

The singer studied her for a long moment, then nodded as though satisfied by what she saw in Karen's face. "Before I get to my news, I'm going to take a step back, okay?"

"Sure." Karen settled into the chair, trying to convey her willingness to listen. "Take your time."

Daria kept her eyes fixed on the tissue she was mauling as she detailed a story of a car accident last winter and the injuries she and her twin sister suffered.

With the exception of inserting exclamations and sounds of dismay and sorrow as the story went along, Karen didn't comment.

When Daria ended the tale, Karen asked, "Where's your sister now?"

Daria's face crumpled. "Darryl said she was dead." This last part was a thin wail.

Karen propelled herself out of the chair and to Daria's side. She gathered the young woman in her arms and hugged her while she cried. Daria's story raised a lot of questions in her mind, and something didn't sit quite right when it came to Darryl. She had an instinctive aversion to the man. He was too slick, and there was a glint of cruelty in his eyes.

Was he telling the truth about Alexis dying? But what would he gain by lying? Karen couldn't figure that out, unless he was trying to torture Daria. But that would affect her performance, which didn't seem wise.

"Why don't you call the hospital?" Karen asked. "Surely they should have notified you as next of kin."

Daria shrank back. "Call them?" She put a shaking hand to her mouth.

Karen wouldn't be eager to call and discuss such a devastating topic as losing a loved one either, but pure fear sparkled in Daria's eyes. Anger hummed in Karen's veins, followed by an urge to confront Darryl. He must have his sister completely cowed, afraid to make a move without his permission. "I'll do it. What's the name of the place?"

It took a little convincing, but finally Daria told her the name and address. They found the number on Karen's cell. She began to dial.

"What are you going to say?" Daria asked anxiously.

Karen shrugged. "Not much. If I have to, I'll tell them that I'm a friend." She listened as the phone rang. When a receptionist picked up, she said, "Alexis Hargreaves's room, please."

Daria was ripping up a new tissue, big eyes fixed on Karen's face.

"Please hold." The receptionist went away. "I'm sorry, but there isn't a patient here by that name."

"But I was told she was staying there—"

"I'm sorry, but I can't provide patient information." *Click.*

Karen stared at her phone in disbelief. "She hung up on me."

To her surprise, Daria grabbed the phone. "Let me try." She hit redial, then went through the same scenario. "This is her sister . . . All right then, where is she?" A moment later, she hung up, her shoulders sagging, and put both hands over her face.

"Did they . . ." Karen was afraid to put it into words. Had they confirmed her sister's death?

"They didn't say anything." Daria picked up the phone again. "I'll call her doctor. Our doctor." She ended up leaving a message, since the doctor was out of town. "Isn't that convenient?" Her tone was bitter. "Well, after tomorrow night's performance, I'm going to go to the hospital and get answers. Surely if she . . . they'd have to tell me, right?"

"Yes, they would," Karen said. "Maybe you should cancel the concert and go there today. This is certainly a priority."

Daria pressed her lips together. "No, I have to wait. I can't tip Darryl off."

Karen had gathered that something was wrong with the situation between Daria and Darryl, but she didn't want to pry. She also felt invested in the outcome. Hopefully, Darryl was wrong and Alexis was okay. Why he'd be so cruel was unfathomable. She definitely didn't like him now. Knowing it was totally inadequate, she said, "Let me know if I can do anything to help, okay?"

"Thanks." Daria gave her a weak smile. "You've been a huge help. I was about ready to . . . I don't know, have a breakdown or something."

"I totally get it. I have a sister too." Karen went to the window and drew the curtain aside. The sultry weather meant there was almost no wind. "Want to go kayaking? It might be a good idea to get out of your room for a while." During her recovery process, she'd learned that forcing herself to go outside or to a new location helped shift her attitude.

"I don't think so," Daria said. But she joined Karen at the window, gazing out at the inviting water. "I've never done that before."

"It's easy, and the boats are stable so you won't tip over." Now that Karen suggested it, she realized she really wanted to go. She could get back to her sketching later, after some fresh air and exercise.

"All right, I'll try it. But let's not go out too far." Daria moved toward the bureau. "Let me change first."

"I'll wait downstairs," Karen said. Then she remembered the note. "Oh, and by the way, you have a flower delivery."

Daria glanced up, a pair of shorts in her hand. "From who?"

"I have no idea. Want me to run down and get them?"

"If you don't mind."

Karen went downstairs and retrieved the flowers. By the time she climbed the stairs again, Daria was standing at the suite door. She was dressed in shorts and a T-shirt.

Daria's eyes lit up. "Wow. That arrangement is amazing." She stood back to let Karen set the flowers down, then grabbed the envelope off the spike. "It's from Abbott. He was at the performance last night."

"The older man you sat with at dinner?" Karen remembered him, struck by his courtly and deferential manner toward his companion.

"That's him. He wants to see me again." Daria furrowed her brow. "Too bad it can't happen. He's a nice guy." She dropped the card into the trash can. "But that's life when you work on the road."

Karen stared at the card, tempted to fish it out and insist Daria keep it. She wanted to tell her that maybe she should give Abbott a chance. Really nice guys didn't come along that often. For some reason, Luke popped into her mind. She laughed to herself. She was nowhere near ready for another relationship, not that he'd given any indication he was interested in her that way.

"Did you put on sunscreen?" she asked Daria. "And grab a hat."

Despite the earlier scolding she'd given herself, Karen kept an eye out for Luke as they made their way to the kitchen for bottled water and more cookies, then down to the dock. If they saw him, she planned to ask him to go kayaking too. He was great at cheering people up—when he wasn't making them mad, she remembered ruefully—and fun to be around. But he was nowhere in sight, and all the kayaks were lined up on the grass.

Daria also seemed to be watching for someone, but she was the opposite, moving skittishly as though hoping not to be noticed. By Darryl, no doubt. Thankfully, they didn't run into him.

"The life jackets and paddles are in the shed," Karen said, showing Daria the ropes. She watched carefully as Daria put on the jacket, making sure she fastened it correctly.

Then they chose two boats and carried them to the water.

Once they launched, Karen gave Daria a brief lesson on how to use the paddle and control the boat.

"I love it already," Daria said, giving a push that set her boat gliding.

Karen smiled. "Told you. Come on. Let's paddle toward town."

They paddled along the shore for a while, moving easily on the placid water, then decided to turn back. Daria couldn't stop smiling, especially at the ducks, who seemed to follow them, quacking and diving. The light breeze, the hazy sun, and the shushing of water against the hulls created an almost hypnotic effect.

"That was wonderful," Daria said as she helped Karen haul her kayak onto the grass. "I'm hooked."

"We'll have to go again," Karen said. "It's a great way to relax."

After they stowed the gear, they gathered the empty water bottles and cookie bags and strolled up to the inn. As the day wore on, the temperature steadily rose, which required that they move very slowly. Karen felt like her inner voice was lethargic too. For once, the urgency that drove her busy brain was still.

She knew from experience that the drive and pressure would be back soon enough. But right now, she allowed herself to wallow in merely being present in the day. Taking time to feel the heat enveloping her body, hear the cicadas buzzing, and breathe in the aroma of green growing things.

Two men sat on the veranda, rocking and chatting, iced tea glasses close to hand. Luke was one of them. Karen recognized his deep, gently rumbling voice even before she clearly saw his face. The other man was Abbott.

Daria's steps hitched, and a fluttering hand went to her hair, scraped back in a ponytail. She wasn't even wearing lipstick.

"Don't worry about it," Karen whispered. "You're gorgeous, all outdoorsy and buff."

Daria laughed. "Thanks, I think. Hopefully, Abbott likes the outdoorsy look."

The appreciation in his eyes seemed to say so. Abbott rose from the rocking chair politely as they approached, the way Southern gentlemen were taught.

Luke followed suit, but Karen suddenly felt shy and kept her eyes averted from his intent gaze. Was she afraid to see what was there? Or was she worried that she wouldn't see anything beyond simple friendliness? She reminded herself that she didn't need the complication.

But when Luke grinned and said, "We've been waiting for you two to get back," she knew it was too late.

For her at least.

17

Daria

Daria's heart gave an unexpected leap when she saw Abbott waiting for her on the veranda. Her plan had been to ignore him, even though he'd sent the beautiful bouquet. She couldn't get involved with anyone, not until her life was straightened out. And probably not even then.

What would Abbott do if he knew the truth about her? That was an easy question to answer.

But despite the warning clanging in her ears, Daria returned his smile. "Abbott, how nice to see you." She climbed the steps of the veranda. "Thank you for the flowers. I love them."

His smile was surprisingly boyish. "You do? I hoped you would." He tugged a rocker forward. "Have a seat."

Daria glanced over at Karen and saw that she was sitting next to Luke. So she sat down, although terribly self-conscious about her sweaty, windblown self. She ran her hand through her hair and tugged the elastic on her ponytail into place.

"Would you like a glass of iced tea?" Abbott asked, standing with his hands on the back of his rocker. "How about you, Karen?"

"I'd love one," Daria said.

"Me too," Karen said.

Daria rocked gently back and forth, feeling totally indolent. She had no idea where Darryl was, and at the moment she didn't care. Oh, the real world and all its problems hovered nearby, ready to pounce again, but just for a few minutes she was going to relax and enjoy her life.

Abbott handed frosty glasses to Daria and Karen and sat down again. Today he wore shorts and a polo shirt and an expensive watch. He was understated, debonair, poised.

And kind. Daria almost swallowed an ice cube when she saw the warmth in his blue eyes, which were bracketed by smile lines.

"Nice day for a paddle," he said. "Almost no wind."

"It was great." Daria's shoulders ached gently from the effort, which had engaged muscles she rarely used. "I think I'm hooked."

"I have a sea kayak," Abbott said. "I enjoy exploring the marshes and islands off the coast."

Karen rocked forward. "Really? Where do you go?"

As they sipped and rocked, Abbott regaled them with tales of his kayaking adventures in the Low Country. He'd even kayaked to Cumberland Island, which held the ruins of a mansion owned by the Carnegie family. The whole island was a park now.

"I'd love to go there sometime," Daria said. The island sounded incredibly romantic and intriguing.

"I'd like to go and paint the scenery," Karen said.

Abbott checked his watch. "It's too far to go today, but perhaps we can arrange a trip soon. Anyone up for a late lunch at The Tidewater?" He motioned toward the dock. "I've got my motorboat. We can ride over that way."

Daria exchanged glances with Karen, who nodded. "That sounds wonderful." She stood. "But I'd like to change first."

"Me too." Karen set her empty glass on the side table and got up. "Meet you down here?"

"We'll be waiting. Don't take long," Abbott said. The tone of his voice indicated that he'd miss Daria more than that he was telling her to hurry.

A giggle burst out of Daria once she and Karen were safely inside.

She felt giddy. Yes, that was the word, old-fashioned as it may be. She took Karen's arm. "I think we have ourselves a couple of beaus," she said, deepening her drawl.

"You think so?" Karen asked. "I mean, anyone can tell that Abbott is enamored but—"

"Luke likes you as more than a friend," Daria whispered, interrupting her. She winked, surprised at how playful she felt. "Trust me."

The young women ran upstairs, giggling.

"What are you wearing?" Karen asked before heading up to the third floor.

"My new dress and sandals. Something cool but pretty," Daria said. The periwinkle-blue dress from Miss Millie's was perfect for this occasion. "What about you?"

"I'm wearing my new dress too," Karen answered with a smile.

Daria changed, then brushed her hair and put on makeup. No time to take a shower and really do her hair, so Abbott would have to accept her as she was. The flip of her stomach told her that he wouldn't mind.

Someone knocked and, thinking it was Karen, she called out, "Come in."

But it was Darryl.

To Daria, it was as though the sunlight dimmed when he walked into the room. "Hey," she said casually. She pretended to focus on fastening her sandals.

"Where are you going, looking so pretty?" Darryl leaned against the doorjamb, hands in his pockets. Despite the casual words and body language, he managed to convey a subtle threat of menace.

Normally, Daria would have cowered, eager to placate him and avert any trouble. But the thought of Abbott gave her courage. "I'm going to lunch with friends."

He straightened, his hands curling into loose fists. "What friends?"

The air of menace intensified as he practically spit out the words.

Daria shrugged, feigning calm. A pulse beat in her throat so hard that surely it must be visible. "Abbott Forbes." She watched him closely, seeing how the anger faded, replaced by calculation.

"Good job." Darryl nodded in approval. "Maybe I can take a second run at him later."

No way. But Daria didn't say anything as she finished buckling her sandal straps. She stood, smoothing the skirt of her new dress. "I'd better go. Abbott is downstairs."

He didn't move.

Daria brushed past Darryl, forcing him to step backward, and paused to pick up her handbag. In the hall, Daria waited for him to emerge, not wanting him to snoop around her room while she was gone. Then she locked the door and hurried down the stairs, all the while conscious of his gaze on her.

At the bottom of the steps, she faltered, gripping the newel post for support. Daria was counting the minutes until she could be free of her half brother. She had no idea what her life would be like when she escaped him, but anything was better than living under his thumb.

Winnie sat behind the desk. She smiled at Daria. "Don't you look lovely? That color is perfect on you."

Daria managed to pull herself together. "Thank you. I'm on my way to lunch with Abbott Forbes."

The older woman clasped her hands together in delight. "That lovely man. He lost his dear wife, oh, about five years ago. We've been hoping he would fall in love again."

Heat rushed up Daria's neck into her cheeks. "Don't be jumping the gun on me. It's just lunch." Wasn't it?

Winnie smiled. "Time will tell. Have a nice day."

Daria returned the pleasantry, but she couldn't shake the feeling that Winnie knew something she didn't. What was it about this place? She patted her handbag, thinking of the tiny Bible Winnie had given her. She carried it everywhere, feeling comforted every time she saw it.

The other three were waiting on the veranda, but Daria had eyes only for Abbott.

His reaction when he saw her was gratifying, the admiration in his eyes unmistakable. He held out an arm. "Ready, milady? Your chariot awaits." He smiled.

Daria laughed, her mood suddenly light. Who knew the dignified Abbott could be playful? She slipped her hand into the crook of his elbow. "Lead on, fine sir."

Abbott's boat was large and sleek, with comfortable seating and a powerful engine.

"I keep this at my father's place," Abbott said. "I'm up here quite often, so it makes sense." He stood at the wheel, with Daria beside him, and navigated the lake with ease. On the way, he pointed out his father's home, a stately manor near the shore. "I grew up there. Magnolia Harbor will always be home."

Home. One of the sweetest words in the world. A pang of longing and homesickness pierced Daria. It had been years since she'd returned to the hollow, to her grandmother's house. Cousins now owned it, and Daria felt as though it wasn't hers any longer.

The noise of the motor made conversation difficult, so Daria spent the short trip gazing out at the shoreline.

Soon they reached The Tidewater's dock, where Abbott tied up with Luke's help. Then the foursome made their way to the restaurant.

"Inside or out?" the hostess asked, clutching tall menus.

Despite the heat of the day, they chose to sit outside, where they could enjoy an unobstructed view of the lake. The umbrella over the table provided shade, and tall fans were whirring to circulate the air.

Conversation was light over lunch, touching on various topics. Daria mostly listened, feeling that any discussion of her life was a minefield. But for a little while she was able to pretend that the accident had never happened. That Darryl hadn't come back into her life. That she hadn't done things that could never be undone. Or forgiven.

For a little while, she was only a young woman out to lunch with friends. A young woman wearing a pretty new dress and accepting adoring glances from a handsome man as her due. He was attentive but not cloyingly so. She had the sense that he was waiting for cues from her, that he wouldn't push her or presume.

That visceral longing rose again. Why couldn't she have a normal life? Why couldn't she have the love of a good man and a home?

Daria lifted a desperate prayer to the heavens. *If it's possible, please.*

18

Grace

By early afternoon, Grace was satisfied with how the inn looked, as far as being clean. She would cut flowers in the morning for arrangements and set up the buffet table with snowy linens and polished silver.

The silver. She sighed as she stood in the kitchen applying polish to each fork, spoon, and knife in the set, one after the other. It was a good thing she had extra containers.

Charlotte glanced over from her mixer, which had been humming all day. "After this batch, I can help you with that, if you want."

"That's all right. I know you're busy." Grace polished a spoon with a soft cloth, admiring the shine of the lustrous metal. There really was nothing like real silver when it came to appearance and function.

Now Charlotte sighed. "I sure am. Besides the ice cream for tomorrow, I'm making a few trays of desserts for Dean. His temporary helpers haven't started yet."

"Wow, that is a lot." Grace raised her eyebrows. "Maybe *I* should help *you*."

Charlotte studied the contents of the bowl. "Ah, no worries. I've got it under control."

Winnie poked her head into the kitchen, her forehead creased in confusion. "Grace, there's a call I think you should take." She pointed at the kitchen phone. "He's on hold."

"What is it about?" Grace asked.

Her aunt shook her head. "Better let him explain." She winced.

"Sorry. I know you're busy, but it sounds urgent."

"All right, I'll take it." Grace wiped her hands on a paper towel and went to the phone, puzzled as to what the caller wanted. Winnie was really good about screening out salespeople and other telemarketing calls that were time wasters. She also was fully trained to take reservations.

"Hello?" Grace said. "This is Grace Porter."

"Connor Benton here." The man's voice was gravelly. "I've got a matter of some urgency that I need to speak to you about."

Grace felt her brow furrow. Was this a trick to get her time and attention? "Can you be more specific, please? I'm in the middle of getting ready for a major event."

He cleared his throat. "I'd rather not discuss it over the phone or come out to your inn. Is there somewhere else we can meet? Or we can do it at my place."

She definitely didn't like the sound of this. "I'm sorry, but you'll need to give me more information than that. And I'm only meeting you in public."

Charlotte's head jerked up, her eyes concerned.

"Of course, of course." Connor paused. "I'm a private investigator. And I'm looking into criminal activity."

"What does that have to do with me?" Grace asked. "Or my inn?"

"I'll give you the details when we meet." He went on to suggest a meeting at his motel on the outskirts of town, where there was a function room he could use. The detective shifted gears. "I'd really appreciate your help, ma'am. My elderly clients are depending on me."

"All right," Grace said with reluctance. "But I'm bringing someone with me. Someone who used to work for the FBI."

Now Charlotte's eyes were like saucers.

Connor laughed. "Good. I'll enjoy meeting him or her. I'll be here all day. Give me a buzz when you have an ETA."

Grace hung up, then untied her apron. "I'd better take care of this now. I hope Spencer can go with me." She reached for the phone.

"Wait," Charlotte said. "What's going on?"

"I don't know," Grace said. "He wouldn't give me any details."

Charlotte frowned. "That sounds ominous."

"I'm sure it's nothing to do with us personally," Grace said. "But I'm not going without Spencer."

Not only did Spencer agree, but he offered to drive.

Shortly after Grace called Connor back, Spencer pulled up in front of the inn in his black Infiniti sedan.

The air-conditioning was blasting, Grace noticed with appreciation as she slid inside. "Thanks for going with me," she said, buckling her seat belt.

Spencer drove around the circle and back out onto the road. "I took the liberty of checking out Mr. Benton. He's a licensed PI in Chicago."

"So he's legit?" Grace laughed at her own question. She was talking like someone on a television show. "That's good to know."

"Any idea what he wants?" Spencer asked. He kept his eyes on the road as they drove along the lake.

Grace gazed out her window, seeing flashes of blue through thick trees. "None. But it must have something to do with the inn and one of my guests. That's what I figure."

They drove the rest of the way in silence. Off the beaten path, the motel was older and somewhat run-down, with a square main building and a wing of double-decker rooms. A few cars were parked in front of the rooms and near the office. The neon sign flickered, and some of the letters were missing.

"I feel like I'm in a noir film," Grace remarked. "A mysterious meeting at a seedy motel."

"Yeah, it's strange all right." Spencer wheeled in and parked in front of the office. He came around and opened the door for Grace, allowing her to cross the office threshold first.

As they entered, a burly man rose from one of the orange vinyl chairs in the reception area. He was dressed neatly in a sport shirt and slacks. "Grace Porter? I'm Connor Benton." He took out his wallet and presented his identification to them.

After they checked his ID, Grace handed it back to him.

Connor turned to the clerk, an elderly woman with beady eyes and fluffy orange hair, and said, "These folks are here to meet with me. We'll be in the back room."

"Want coffee or iced tea?" the woman asked, studying them. At their polite declines, she returned to the newspaper she had been reading.

Connor grabbed a file folder off the occasional table, then led the way through a door to a hallway. At the very end was a room with stacks of chairs and a few long tables set up. "This used to be a restaurant, I understand," he said. "Now local groups meet here."

None Grace was involved with, but that didn't mean anything. She scanned the banners around the walls for various fraternal organizations. Without invitation, she pulled out a chair at the closest table and sat.

Spencer took a seat beside her, and Connor went to the other side of the table and set the folder down.

"So what's this about, Mr. Benton?" Spencer said after introducing himself. "We don't want to take a lot of your time."

Connor's mouth quirked. With his wide head and thickset neck, he had the appearance of a bulldog. "Nor do you want to waste yours. I get it." He opened the folder and extracted two photographs, then slid them across the table. "Do you recognize these folks?"

Grace felt her jaw drop in shock and disbelief when she recognized Daria and Darryl. "I do. They're guests at the inn." She pointed. "She's a singer, and he's her accompanist."

Connor nodded. "They're performing at your music fest, right?"

"Yes, they are." Grace continued to stare at the photographs as if they could tell her more, but they looked like typical publicity stills. "She seems like a very nice young woman."

"What have they done?" Spencer asked, his voice somber. "I'm guessing you didn't come all the way from Chicago to catch a show."

"I see you've done your homework," the detective told Spencer. "No, I'm not here for a show, although I've heard that Miss Hargreaves has a spectacular voice. That's a shame because she won't have much chance to use it in jail."

Grace gasped. "Jail? No way." She couldn't imagine beautiful, sweet Daria as a criminal. Sadness followed her shock. She hated to hear bad things about people she liked.

Connor tapped the flat of his hand on the table. "I'm afraid that they've been implicated in a theft of precious jewelry. My clients hosted them at a party in their home. After the event, my clients realized some items had gone missing." He pulled out two more photographs from the folder and slid them across the table. "Just in case you might have seen these."

Grace studied the jewelry. "No, I'm afraid not. We don't snoop in guest rooms, you know."

"Of course not," Connor said easily. "But I thought Miss Hargreaves might have worn the jewelry during a performance."

"Why haven't your clients gone to the police?" Spencer asked. "I'm not sure what we can do to help you." He glanced at Grace. "She isn't going to search their luggage or vehicle for you."

"My clients filed a report, but there were no leads," Connor explained. "I believe they asked me to look into it because the necklace is a family heirloom. Anyway, I've been investigating Darryl and Daria Hargreaves, and I've discovered an interesting pattern."

Grace's heart began to thud with dread. She had an idea where he was headed. "Go on."

"In almost every place they've been, a patron has filed a police report regarding stolen valuables," Connor continued. "Once is interesting. Twice might be a coincidence. But half a dozen times? It's clear they're professionals."

Spencer's warning to her after Julep's necklace was stolen flashed into her mind. Grace turned to him and saw the agreement in his expression. "We've had a couple of things go missing recently," she said. She gave Connor the details.

"Did they file police reports?" Connor asked.

"I'm not sure," Grace said. "I don't think Luke has yet, and Julep's necklace was stolen or lost at another inn. You'd have to check with her or the innkeeper."

Connor noted the information on a piece of paper. "You're only confirming my theory that the Hargreaves are working in Magnolia Harbor. So what I'd like to do is stage a sting at your place tomorrow night."

Spencer shook his head. "Hold on. I'm not sure that's such a good idea."

"If I could come up with something better, I would," Connor said. "But tomorrow night is very high-profile, right? From what I understand, there will be a lot of well-heeled guests attending."

Grace gasped again. "And *Low Country Life* magazine will be there. I can't let them find out that we may have been housing a pair of thieves." She put her hands up to her face, appalled by the situation. She didn't want Daria and Darryl to steal from her neighbors and friends, but she didn't want the inn's reputation dragged through the mud either. This was an impossible situation.

Connor nodded. "I hear you. That's why it's going to be a covert operation. We'll let the duo work the room, and then we'll stop them afterward."

"We?" Spencer asked, his tone sharp. "Who else is on your team?"

The detective's smile was smug. "Why, the local force, of course. A few officers are going to be attending undercover. Once I explained the situation to Captain Daley, he was on board."

"Are you okay with this?" Spencer asked Grace.

"Not really," Grace admitted. "But I don't see a choice. Tomorrow night is their last performance in town. They're checking out the next day." She thought again about the magazine team. "Can you do the arrest after the magazine people leave? Maybe Dean can lure them away to The Tidewater or something."

"We'll try," Connor said. "The captain is also worried about negative publicity, since Magnolia Harbor depends so much on tourists. It's unfortunate that a couple of bad apples can spoil a place. But we have to end this crime spree as soon as possible."

"Can we warn people?" Grace asked. Otherwise, the inn guests would be sitting ducks. She didn't like the idea of that.

Connor made a scoffing sound. "That would defeat the whole purpose. They won't get away with stealing this time, so any loss will be temporary."

Grace mulled over the situation. She could refuse, but then the pair might steal something and go on their merry way unhindered, free to rob someone else. "You're sure that Darryl and Daria are the thieves?"

"Sure as I can be, without catching them red-handed," Connor said. "And that's what we plan to do. Get 'em with their hands in the cookie jar, so to speak."

Grace exchanged glances with Spencer. "What do you think?"

He waved a hand. "As long as there's backup, I don't see a problem. I'll keep my eyes open too. The point is to witness something, right?

So you have a reason to search them?"

"That's the plan." Connor played with his shirt collar. "I've had lots of training about pickpockets and the like. One of the officers or I will always be within sight of both of them."

"Add me to the roster," Spencer said. "I've had some training too."

"You're former FBI, aren't you?" Connor asked.

Spencer nodded.

"Welcome aboard. I'll let the captain know." Connor slid the photographs and his notes into the folder and closed it. "See you tomorrow evening."

Grace waited until they were safely in the car and away before speaking. "I just can't wrap my head around this. Daria seems like such a sweet young woman."

"I know, but many criminals are charming. That's how they get away with their misdeeds." Spencer adjusted the air-conditioning. "Cool enough?"

"Fine, thanks." Grace leaned her elbow on the armrest and gazed out at the countryside whipping past. She had to admit that her confidence in humanity was shaken. She and Charlotte opened their doors to guests in good faith. Realizing that two of them were taking advantage of their hospitality and trust made her feel ill.

Spencer seemed to pick up on her funk and remained silent.

As he neared the drive to the inn, she reached out and touched his arm. "Let's go for a ride. I'm not ready to go back yet."

She never did this, never shirked her responsibilities. But right now, she needed time and space to think, to adjust her attitude.

Without answering, Spencer hit the gas, and they sped by the inn entrance.

Grace craned her neck to look down the drive, feeling guilty. But surely Charlotte and Winnie could hold down the fort a little longer.

He took her out of Magnolia Harbor and into the countryside. They drove along winding country roads shaded with live oaks or abutting wide fields. The peaceful vistas soothed Grace's stormy emotions and released the knot in her belly.

A small store cropped up suddenly, one of those ancient places stenciled with advertisements for goods. An ice cooler stood on the porch, along with a row of rusted metal chairs. Gas pumps from another era still stood in front, merely a curiosity now.

Spencer turned into the parking lot.

"What are you doing?" Grace asked.

"Getting us cold drinks," Spencer said. He left the car running while he went inside, returning with two icy soda bottles. He popped off the tops and handed one to Grace.

"Thanks."

Spencer took off again. Soon he parked in front of an old clapboard church surrounded by a cemetery. He opened his door. "Want to take a stroll?"

Grace followed him into the cemetery, sipping on her soda as she read the headstones, noting the names and dates. So many short lives. Birds chirped in the trees and bushes and hopped along the grass. In one corner, where the stones were blackened and leaning, the grass was mainly moss, deep and velvety soft underfoot. Utter peace settled over the timeless spot.

They wound their way to the largest monument, a small building on a rise. Brass plaques on the marble listed the family members who were interred inside.

"My grandparents are buried in a cemetery like this," Spencer said. "They had a farm, and the family lived there for generations."

Grace absorbed this, comparing it to her own history. "That's how it is for us here. My ancestors settled in Magnolia Harbor." The reminder of her family's long history gave Grace courage. Yes, she was facing a difficult situation. But with the help of her family and friends and a little faith, she and the inn would make it through okay.

She drank the last sweet drops of soda. "I'm ready to go back now, if you are."

19

Karen

Karen sat on a rocking chair on the veranda, sipping coffee. This early in the day, the air was still relatively cool. Thunderstorms were predicted for later, and she hoped they would actually arrive.

Tension was definitely building in the atmosphere, making people snippy and irritable. Even the lovely ladies of the inn seemed on edge. They were hosting a huge event tonight, so maybe that was the cause of their stress.

The screen door opened behind her, and she turned to see Luke emerging, also holding a mug. He grinned when their eyes met, and her stomach flipped.

After lunch the day before, which had been a blast, she'd used her painting as an excuse to escape his company. And then she'd avoided him ever since. Thankfully, he'd had dinner with his colleagues last night, which had made it easier.

"Hey, Luke." She faced the view again, sipping calmly, acting like her pulse wasn't racing. At least she hoped it appeared that way. Her lip curled. So much for her resolution to move slowly the next time. Although thus far, it appeared to be a totally one-sided relationship. She intended to keep it that way.

"Hey, Karen. Nice day." He eased into the adjacent rocker and began moving it slowly, pushing off with his feet. "I can't believe it's over eighty already."

She rocked too. "Thunderstorms later, they said."

"So I heard. There's a severe thunderstorm warning posted for this county."

"It could be bad. Hope we don't get a tornado." Hysterical laughter bubbled in Karen's chest, and it took all her effort to swallow it. They sounded exactly like two old-timers on a park bench with nothing better to do than talk about the weather.

Without her saying a word or even releasing a giggle, Luke burst into laughter.

That set the floodgates loose, and she joined in.

After a few moments, he wiped a finger under his streaming eyes. "I'm not even sure what we're laughing about. Are you?"

"Not really," Karen admitted. The strain she'd been feeling dissolved. "What are you doing today?"

He rocked. "Unfortunately, I've got meetings."

Her spirits sank a little. Had she been too forward? "I'll probably do some painting and go for a swim. It's too hot to kayak."

"A swim? That sounds great." Luke leaned his head against the rocker back. "How about later? Want to attend the concert with me?"

Karen's spirits bobbed back up, like a ball in water. "Sure. But aren't we kind of doing that already, since we're both staying here?" She bit her lip. *Shut up and stop being logical.*

Luke turned to her. "Yes, but I meant *with* me. Like a date." He enunciated every word clearly as if he wanted to be sure she understood.

A date. Was she ready? Apparently so, because she found herself nodding. "I'd like that."

He appeared relieved. "Great. Meet you in the lobby? We can eat together."

Karen smiled. "Sounds good."

After swallowing the rest of the coffee in his mug, Luke jumped out of the chair. "Have a great day. I know I will." Whistling, he headed for the screen door and slipped inside.

Now Karen leaned back against the seat. She actually had a date. For a moment, she reveled in happiness and anticipation.

Although the two men were equally good-looking and intelligent, Luke was the exact opposite of Joshua. Luke was humble, kind, and funny. Joshua had definitely lacked a sense of humor, especially about himself. That should have been a red flag.

A thought struck, making her sit upright again. What was she going to wear? She'd already worn her new green linen dress to The Tidewater. Should she go on another shopping trip to Miss Millie's?

She grinned. Absolutely.

Luke was waiting for Karen as she descended the stairs that evening. Next to him, the front door was opening to admit more guests, and others were milling about the public rooms. She'd heard that a hundred people would be here tonight.

Wearing a dinner jacket and a bow tie, Luke stood with his hands in his pockets, watching the crowd around him. His dress shirt was blinding white, making a nice contrast to his tanned skin and dark hair.

Karen paused on the landing. Luke was so handsome, it stole her breath. She gazed her fill, then tweaked the full skirt of her new cocktail dress into place and started descending again. The fabric was purple rayon with lace as an overlay on the bodice and forming the long sleeves. She'd been hesitant about the color, but Sophie Mah, the owner of the dress shop, had insisted it was perfect for her.

From the admiring glances she was getting, it seemed Sophie was right.

As for Luke, his mouth actually dropped open when he saw Karen on the stairs. "You look great."

She twirled a little, letting her skirt swish. "Thanks. So do you."

He held out an arm, and she took his elbow, enjoying how feminine and cared for that made her feel. They made their way across the foyer and outside, walking down the lantern-lit path through the gardens to the barn. Here they would eat dinner, then return to the house for the concert.

As they strolled along the path, Karen noticed Daria and Abbott ahead. They were also walking arm in arm and seemed very happy together. Daria's creepy brother, Darryl, was lurking behind the pair, walking close by as though eavesdropping.

Thank goodness neither Karen nor Luke had any nosy relatives around, although hers were quite the opposite. She'd sent Emma a picture of herself in the purple dress and mentioned the date. Emma's message had been all smiling faces and hearts. She was such a dear.

Inside the barn, festive with draped lights and swags of fabric, they joined the line waiting to eat. As it moved slowly, Karen soaked in the atmosphere, observing how the subtle lighting flattered people's faces. She spotted Julep, Spencer, Dean, and other people now familiar to her. What an amazing place Magnolia Harbor was, that it could spark such deep connections so quickly.

"This is a really nice event," Luke said. He fiddled with a cuff link. "And kind of fun having a reason to dress up."

"I hear you," Karen said. "I almost never wear a dress." Standing close to him as she was, she could smell his woodsy aftershave.

"That's a shame," he said, his eyes teasing. "You've been depriving us."

Karen felt a blush start somewhere around her collarbone. She turned and grabbed a plate off the stack to hide her embarrassment.

She hefted a fork and realized it was silver. *Nice.* The innkeepers really knew how to throw a party.

The buffet offered an array of cold meats, seafood, and salads, a nod to the hot weather. Karen helped herself to shrimp, tossed and quinoa salads, and a sweet potato biscuit that was still warm. Then she waited for Luke, and together they found seats at an empty table.

She'd been hoping some of her new acquaintances would join them, but Osgood and the other astronomy professors arrived first. Luke sent her an apologetic look, but she smiled in return. Nothing was going to put her in a bad mood tonight. And at least she could focus on her delicious meal while they talked shop.

As she expected, the men discussed astronomy and the meetings they had all attended that day.

"Perkins is a good theorist, but sometimes he overreaches." Osgood faced Luke and lifted a brow. "There's a lesson in there somewhere. Take it under advisement."

Seated beside Karen, Luke shifted in his seat, his spine straightening. For a long moment, he regarded the older man with narrowed eyes. Then he threw his napkin on the table, a gesture similar to throwing down the gauntlet.

The other men watched, one with a glass halfway to his lips, another with his knife and fork poised above his plate.

"How about you take something under advisement, Osgood?" Luke didn't raise his voice, which only made his words all the more menacing. "If we can't come to terms on my continued employment in your department, I'll be leaving. In fact, I have several irons in the fire already."

One of the other men chortled. "Guess he told you, old boy," he muttered.

Osgood glared at his colleague. Then he set his utensils down and raised both hands. "I didn't mean anything by it," he told Luke. "It was merely an observation."

Luke remained silent as he stared at Osgood.

"About Perkins, I mean," Osgood added. He picked up his utensils again. "You do good work, Luke. Very good work indeed." Keeping his gaze on his plate, he said, "We'll firm up your continued employment when we return to the university."

Karen reached under the table and squeezed Luke's hand briefly. He'd won.

Luke squeezed back and sent her a covert smile. Then he deftly changed the subject to something Osgood knew about, thereby smoothing over the scene.

What a guy. He certainly had social chops. Karen half listened to the conversation, content to absorb the atmosphere and the meal. She wasn't able to eat much due to the excited knot in her stomach, another symptom she recognized.

They were almost finished with dinner when her phone beeped. More out of curiosity than anything, she checked for messages. Her lips curved in a wry smile. Joshua, with impeccable timing. Had he sensed that she was getting over him and moving on? She could believe it since the man had uncanny skills in that department.

"Something good?" Luke asked, his gaze innocently inquiring.

Karen pressed the command to block. Delete all texts? Yes. Once finished, she smiled at her date. "Oh yeah. It's all good."

The weight of her relationship with Joshua slid off her back, exactly as if it were a smothering cloak bogging her down. She felt free and light, like a balloon soaring to the sky.

After the meal, Karen and Luke strolled back to the inn along another lantern-lit path leading through the gardens. The night was sultry, tree frogs chirping away. As they paused by the rose garden to admire the blossoms, a sudden breeze kicked up and the frogs stopped singing.

"They must know something we don't," Karen said with a laugh.

"It feels like that storm is coming in," Luke said, brushing at his windblown hair. "Hopefully, it will cool things off."

"We'd better get inside, then." Karen glanced around. In the west, clouds were racing to cover the star-strewn sky. She hoped the storm would hold off until after the performance so the musicians wouldn't be competing with thunder and lightning right overhead.

They joined the throng of guests crossing the veranda and entering the music room, where chairs had been set up. Double doors were open wide to allow for traffic flow and to enlarge the space. Karen and Luke found seats near the back, leaving the ones up front for others.

A string quartet was warming up while Daria stood nearby chatting with Abbott and Julep. According to the program, Daria would perform selections from Mozart, Handel, and others with the musicians. So Darryl had the night off.

Karen found herself searching the crowd for him, hoping he wasn't here. After she'd witnessed Daria's torment, her distaste for the man had hardened into dislike. She also wondered if Daria had heard from her doctor. What happened to Alexis was a troubling puzzle. Karen prayed she was all right.

With the unspoken signals governing most crowds, the audience began to settle into their seats.

Julep held up a gong and struck it, and everyone quieted.

Grace stepped forward, looking lovely in a pink silk dress. "Good evening and welcome to Magnolia Harbor Inn. I trust you enjoyed your dinner. The wonderful Edible Delights catered it for us."

The onlookers cheered and clapped, revealing their enthusiasm and appreciation for the fine food.

Once they settled, Grace said, "And for dessert we have homemade ice cream from our own kitchen. Charlotte, please take a bow."

Standing on the edge of the crowd, Charlotte waved and smiled. She was beautiful in a blue print dress with a full skirt.

The crowd applauded.

"We'll be serving dessert after the performance. So let's get started. Tonight you'll be hearing from . . ." Grace went on to give brief descriptions of the performances, which would conclude with Jerzy Flynn, famed mandolin player.

Luke leaned closer. "I've heard of him," he said behind his hand. "His music is really eclectic."

"I have too," Karen said. "I listened to an interview with him on the radio." She sat back in the chair, grateful it was padded instead of metal, and prepared to listen.

The lights dimmed while those focused near the musicians brightened.

As the string quartet played the first piercing notes, their sheer beauty raised goose bumps on Karen's arms. And when Daria began to sing, her pure voice and the instruments wove together, harmony and counterpoint, lifting the audience into an enchanted realm.

At Daria's last note, the crowd went wild.

Cheeks flushing pink, the singer took numerous bows with the string quartet. Then they slipped out of the performance area and made way for the next musicians on cello and piano.

After another great performance, Jerzy Flynn took the stage. He was a squat man with squinty eyes, tufted hair, and a dry drawl. He was in need of a shave too. But when he sat down and began to play, the listeners were transported to the Appalachian hills and beyond.

Karen was startled to find moisture spring to her eyes. The music was so evocative, creating images of country roads winding through rolling hills, of smoke drifting from chimneys and welcoming the listener home.

Across the room, Daria stood near Abbott, and Karen witnessed her wiping away a tear or two also. Daria had grown up in Tennessee, she remembered.

She was also a friend. Karen hoped they would stay in touch once they went their separate ways. Of course, Karen wasn't sure where she'd be living. But for once, the thought didn't cause anxiety to gnaw. She could allow her next steps to slowly unfold one by one.

Tonight she was listening to an amazing concert with a wonderful man and staying in a gorgeous place. Tonight was incredible. She trusted that tomorrow would be too.

When Jerzy finished, the audience applauded and gave the man a standing ovation.

"That was fantastic," Karen said to Luke. "I loved every minute this evening."

Luke smiled. "So did I. And guess what? It's not over." He gestured to where servers were bringing out carts to the living room. "There's ice cream."

Thunder rumbled in the distance.

"And there's the storm," Karen added. "Perfect timing."

The crowd milled around, the chatter of voices deafening, even with such high ceilings.

Luke guided Karen through the throng toward the dessert station.

Charlotte stood near the array, supervising as the helpers arranged metal tubs on ice in a similar setup to a gelato shop. Placards in front identified the flavors, and an array of toppings was lined up.

"We'll get a few pictures of the table," a woman with bright-red lipstick and matching nails said. She was impeccably groomed from her blonde hair to her expensive stilettos. "You ready, Tony?"

A photographer standing nearby nodded. "All set, Celia."

"Thanks again for featuring us," Grace said, joining the small group. "We're around tomorrow if you want to do any follow-up interviews or photographs. We'll be putting the public rooms back in order in the morning."

"Good, good." Celia cocked her head, still studying the dessert table. "We were disappointed not to be able to stay here, but thankfully The Tidewater could accommodate us. We're going to give the inn a mention."

"Dean will be happy to hear that," Charlotte said. "We all consider it a plum to be referenced in *Low Country Life*."

Karen had seen the glossy lifestyle magazine at the inn. How wonderful that Grace and Charlotte were being featured. They certainly deserved it. Then she noticed Daria standing alone in a corner, a rare moment for the popular performer. Karen excused herself, leaving Luke watching as the photographer went to work.

Karen gave the young woman a spontaneous hug. "You were spectacular."

"Thank you." Daria's return hug was warm. "You've been such a great friend."

Karen laughed. "I was just thinking that about you. Let's stay in touch."

To her surprise, Daria's lips began to tremble. She blinked rapidly, as though ready to burst into tears.

"What's wrong?" Karen asked, alarmed. Had Daria gotten bad news about her sister?

Biting her bottom lip, Daria shook her head. "Sorry. I can't talk about it." Distracted by a man walking past, she touched Karen's arm. "Is that the police officer we saw downtown?"

Karen studied the man, who was burly and had a buzz cut, like the officer they'd seen. But it was hard to tell because the man was out of uniform and dressed to the nines like everyone else. "I'm not sure."

"It looks like him." Daria's gaze followed the man for a moment. Then she gave Karen a wan smile and a brief hug. "Thank you for everything. You've been more wonderful than you know." With that enigmatic statement, Daria pushed through the people standing nearby and disappeared into the crowd.

Luke appeared at Karen's side. "The magazine people left so they're ready to start serving ice cream." Then he noticed her expression. "Is everything okay?"

Karen shrugged. "Not really, but there isn't anything I can do." She rested a hand on his arm and pulled him closer, not wanting anyone to overhear. "It's Daria. I'm concerned about her."

"Is there a problem with Abbott?" Luke asked. "I'm sorry to hear that. They seemed so happy together."

Luke didn't know anything about Daria's twin sister or her unpleasant brother, Karen realized, and this wasn't the time or the place to explain. Plus, she wasn't sure these personal topics were appropriate to share. Now she regretted saying anything.

"I'm not sure what's wrong. Maybe I can catch up with her tomorrow before she checks out." She slipped her hand into his. "Let's have dessert."

Then the lights went out. And the house was engulfed in total darkness.

Grace

Grace had just closed the front door behind Celia, Tony, and Dean when the inn lost electricity. Her first reaction was shock, followed by a burst of gratitude for two things. First, that the interview had gone well, without the *Low Country Life* team learning of the impending sting operation. And second, that she'd installed an emergency exit light in the foyer. Immediately after the power failed, the glowing red light switched on like clockwork.

In the other room, people screamed in surprise, followed by a murmur of voices.

Grace quickly crossed to the desk, where she kept emergency battery-powered lanterns and flashlights. They could also light the decorative candles set around the public rooms. Losing power didn't happen often here, but it wasn't totally unexpected with the storms they got.

As though hearing her thoughts, the wind began to howl around the building and lightning flashed, illuminating the tall windows. A few seconds later, thunder boomed. The thunderstorm had arrived in full force.

"Grace, what happened?" Spencer stood in the doorway to the living room, the pinpoint beam from his phone cutting through the dark.

"The storm, I'm assuming." Grace switched on one of the lanterns and set it on the desk. Now she could dig out the flashlights. She handed Spencer the other lantern. "Would you please take that into the living room for me?"

"Sure. Charlotte was lighting some candles when I left. People are figuring out they can use these too." He waved his cell phone around. "Pretty handy."

"Until the battery dies," Grace said. She opened a deep drawer and pawed through it. Cleaning out the drawer was going to be a top priority once she had a minute to spare.

"Be right back," Spencer said. His shoes clicked along the marble floor as he strode off on his mission.

Grace had found the flashlights by the time he returned, with Captain Keith Daley in tow.

"The inn is the only place without power," Daley said. "I checked in with the power company and our dispatcher." Dark-skinned and bald, the captain wore his dinner jacket with authority and grace, as if he were still in uniform.

"So it's not the storm?" Grace asked. "But I assumed it was." She winced when a thunderbolt crashed, making the mansion shake.

"So did I," Spencer said. "We're going to check the main."

"That's right," the captain put in. "If it were only one circuit we blew, the rest of the lights would be still be on. So the whole system went down."

Connor Benton dashed into the foyer. "What's going on? Why did the lights go out?"

"We're going to find out," Daley said. "Hold on."

The private detective glanced around, almost wildly, his hands clenched in loose fists. "Have any of you seen Darryl or Daria lately?"

An alarm rang in Grace's mind. "I haven't, and I've been out here for at least ten minutes."

Connor groaned. "Last time I saw them was right before the lights went out." He turned to Daley. "Daria was talking to one of your guys, the one with a buzz cut."

"Well, he's probably got it under control then," the captain said, then motioned to Spencer. "Ready?"

Grace handed Spencer one of the flashlights. "I hope it's something simple." She'd thought about installing a backup generator in the past, but for a building this size, it was a huge investment. And power outages were rare. Inconvenient but rare.

The two men headed for the utility room.

Grace decided to check on her guests in the living room. She switched on the other lantern and picked it up, then grabbed a flashlight. "Coming, Connor?"

He hesitated. "I'd rather wait here, if you don't mind." He pointed toward the front door. "Just in case."

"Actually, that's a good idea," Grace said. If anyone wanted to sneak out of a building, the perfect time to do so would be when it was shrouded in darkness. "I'll be in the living room if you need me."

The thunderstorm continued to rage, but in the living room, all appeared cozy and bright. Candles glowed on many of the surfaces, illuminating the faces of guests as they chattered and laughed in small groups. Although the crowd had thinned, no one seemed eager to leave, which was perhaps due to the heavy rain. Over at the ice cream table, servers were still filling dishes for guests, who then added their own toppings. In fact, it appeared that many were going back for seconds.

Grace approached Charlotte, who was supervising the servers. "How's it going?"

"Great," Charlotte said. "Everyone was a little shocked at first, but now I think they're having a good time."

"I'm glad Celia and Tony were already gone," Grace said with a shudder. "I certainly don't want a power outage mentioned in our article."

Charlotte put a hand on Grace's arm and drew her into a corner, well away from listening ears. "How's everything else going?"

Grace knew what she was referring to. She'd filled Charlotte and Winnie in after her meeting with Connor the day before. "I'm not sure." She glanced around the room but didn't spot Daria or Darryl. She whispered in Charlotte's ear, asking her if she knew where they were.

Charlotte's eyes flared with alarm. She shook her head. "Not since right before we lost power."

The chandeliers came on with a bright blare, startling the crowd.

Someone started clapping, and others joined in.

"Turn the lights back off," a man called out. "I look better by candlelight."

Everyone laughed.

Spencer and Daley entered the room near where Grace and Charlotte were standing.

"The main was switched off," Spencer said. "On purpose, no doubt."

"Who could have done that?" A terrible sinking feeling of dread told Grace the answer.

A shout went up in the other room. "My mandolin is gone!"

"That's my cue." The captain gave a piercing whistle and gestured to Officers Morris White, Brittany Holmes, and Greg Warshaw, then trotted toward the dining room.

The guests continued to chatter, but concern and confusion replaced their former high spirits.

Grace followed the captain and Spencer, her heart in her throat. Jerzy's mandolin was an extremely valuable and rare instrument.

The performers—with the exception of Daria and Darryl—were gathered in the dining room, clustered around a distraught Jerzy.

Connor bolted into the room and skidded to a stop, eyeing the situation with consternation.

"Look at that," Jerzy said, pointing at a battered case on the dining room table, the lid hanging open. "That is not my instrument."

Grace peered inside, and even she, far from an expert, could tell it wasn't the same mandolin Jerzy had played that evening.

"Take me through what happened," Captain Daley said, then turned to his three officers. "While we're talking, search the building. Do a quick sweep, and then we'll go through it again more thoroughly later."

"Wait," Grace said. "I can go with them with my master key. The guest rooms are probably locked."

"I can do it," Winnie offered. Patting her pocket for her keys, she accompanied the officers out of the room.

But before the captain could ask Jerzy anything, Abbott entered the room, his face ashen. "Why did Daria leave so suddenly?" He turned to Jerzy. "Surely she's not implicated in the theft of your instrument."

Daley moved slowly but with authority toward the banker. "I'm sorry, but we can't discuss an ongoing case. If you give me a call tomorrow, we can talk then. Maybe I'll have some information I can tell you."

Abbott ducked his head, his expression absolutely shattered. "You think Daria had something to do with it." He put a shaking hand to his mouth. "But I refuse to believe it. She's a wonderful young woman, so talented, intelligent, and kind."

Grace's heart went out to the man. Obviously, he had fallen hard for Daria. This situation must be a terrible shock, as if rose-colored glasses had been ripped away to reveal a scene of unparalleled ugliness.

"You were with Daria all night, weren't you, Abbott?" she asked gently.

The captain pursed his lips in surprise at the interruption, but he didn't object. He probably didn't know that Daria had been seeing Abbott.

"Most of it," Abbott said. "After her performance. But then later on, I got caught up talking about business, and she excused herself to mingle. Of course I thought she should." His laugh was bitter. "If I'd known what was going to happen, I never would have let her out of my sight."

"None of us would." Daley's voice was kind. He clapped Abbott on the shoulder. "Why don't you go on back to your dad's house and get some rest? We'll be in touch."

Abbott nodded and shuffled away.

Grace hoped that he would be able to rest. She promised herself she'd check in on him, offer friendship and a listening ear.

The captain waited until Abbott was out of earshot, then said to Jerzy, "So tell me what happened."

The musician ran his hands through his hair, disarranging it even more. "I don't know. When the performance was over, I placed my instrument in here with the others. After that business with the lights, well, I thought I should check on it. And I saw this." He waved a hand at the case. "My mandolin is an antique, but this one is old junk."

"Okay, got it," Daley said. "I'll take an official statement in a bit. But first we need to control the scene." He whirled around. "Spencer, Connor, can you help me? We have to talk to the other guests. I don't want anyone walking out yet." He let out a slight groan. "We're going to need backup. Every car must be searched too."

"Can we leave soon?" one of the string musicians asked. "We've got a three-hour drive."

"Soon, I promise," the captain said. "In the meantime, please open your instrument cases and put them on the table for me to inspect."

Grace didn't know much about crime scenes, but she guessed this was a nightmare of one. Some people had begun to filter out after the concert, but there must be more than fifty people still in the building. Daley was also being extremely thorough. While no one doubted that Daria and her brother had stolen the mandolin, he wasn't making that assumption.

The three men went into the living room, and Grace heard the captain addressing the crowd. He told them to be patient, that he'd have them on their way shortly.

"I'm going to put the ice cream in the freezer before it turns to soup," Charlotte told Grace. "The rest of the catering staff already left ages ago, and I'd like to let my helpers go home."

"That's fine. But maybe see if people want anything else first. Food and drink always help." Grace thought of something. "Actually, I'll go put on a pot of coffee and get out some cookies." She needed to do something, anything, to keep her hands busy.

The kitchen felt like a sanctuary, a spot of peace during an upsetting evening. Grace went through the automatic actions of putting a filter in the basket, then spooning in coffee.

She was at the sink filling the glass carafe when she heard a knock at the back door, startling her so much that she almost dropped the fragile container. What was that? Surely someone wasn't out there in this weather. It must have been a branch blown by the wind. Or a stray garbage can or a plant pot rolling around.

Stephanie, one of the servers, pushed a laden cart into the kitchen. "I'm going to put all this away."

"Thanks," Grace said. "We appreciate your help."

The knocking sounded again.

Grace set the carafe safely down, wondering if she should go investigate. Where was Winston when she needed him? She'd left him safely in her quarters tonight. She didn't want to have to worry about his whereabouts in a big crowd. Not that he was much of a guard dog, but still . . .

"Sounds like someone's knocking," Stephanie said. "Want me to get it?"

Grace wiped her hands on a cloth. "No, I'll go." Taking a deep breath, she went down the short hallway to the door. As she drew closer, she saw that someone was indeed at the door. She could see an oval face framed by a hood. Judging by the figure's height and size, it was a woman.

Then her steps hitched. She knew that face. Grace hurried to unlock and open the door. "Daria, what—" Her words cut off when the visitor pushed down her dripping wet hood.

The young woman resembled Daria, but it wasn't her. Not unless she'd cut six inches off her hair and removed her makeup in the last hour.

"I'm Alexis. Her sister. I understand she's staying here?"

21

Grace

Grace stepped back, realizing she was staring rudely. "Please come in. I didn't know Daria had a sister." She'd leave the revelation that Daria had left the inn for later, in case Alexis knew something important.

Alexis stepped inside and shed her jacket. She held it out to Grace apologetically. "I'm sorry. I wasn't expecting a downpour."

"No problem." Grace hung the coat on a peg. "Neither were we." She ushered Alexis down the hallway. "I'm Grace Porter, the innkeeper. Would you like something to eat or drink? We have leftovers from dinner or a dessert, whatever you like. Cold drinks, hot coffee." She realized she was babbling, trying to put off questions she didn't want to answer.

Alexis gazed around the kitchen. "This place is great." She ran her hand along the countertop. "I love to cook. It must be heaven working in here."

"We like it. My sister is a chef. She's also my business partner." Grace flitted over to the coffeepot. It was almost done brewing. She gestured to a stool. "Please have a seat."

The young woman perched. "I'll take a cup of coffee. Maybe you can tell Daria I'm here?"

To Grace's relief, Karen walked into the kitchen. When she saw Alexis, her mouth dropped open. Then she closed it firmly. "You must be Alexis." She bustled over to Daria's sister and shook her hand. "I've heard so much about you."

Alexis tilted her head. "Really? I hope it was good."

"Of course." Karen waved a hand. "Grace, I'll hang out here for a minute if you want to go talk to Charlotte." She turned to Alexis. "She's Grace's sister."

"The chef?" Alexis asked.

"That's right." The coffee was finally done, so Grace poured Alexis a mug. "Karen, can you get out the cream? Sugar is on the counter. Thanks." Grace hurried from the room, flustered from the effort of hiding information from Alexis. Subterfuge was not her forte.

Out in the foyer, Officers Holmes and White were talking to guests, taking their names and contact information.

"The captain's in the music room," Holmes said to Grace.

Daley was standing in the music room with Spencer and Connor. "Ah, there you are," the captain said when Grace walked in. "We took over this room. Hope you don't mind."

"Of course not. Whatever you need." Grace inhaled deeply. "I've got some news. Daria's twin sister, Alexis, just showed up."

The three men stared at her for a moment.

Finally, Daley asked, "Does she know anything?"

"I don't think so," Grace said. "She's looking for Daria. So did they leave?"

"It appears so," the captain said. "They're not in the building anywhere. But the strange thing is, their rental car is still in the lot. Winnie gave us the registration information, and it matches."

Grace cringed. Had they stolen her car? They could have made copies of her keys. She certainly didn't lock them up.

"They obviously had another method of transport," Spencer said. "I checked, and your car and Charlotte's are still here."

Grace sagged at this good news, but then another disturbing thought struck her. "Did they steal someone else's car?"

"We won't know until all the guests leave," Daley said. "My backup arrived, so I have a couple of officers outside checking vehicles while people are questioned by the officers inside."

Spencer cupped one elbow, rubbing his chin. "Most newer cars have alarms and can't be hot-wired. So I'm curious to find out what happened."

"You and me both." The captain clasped both hands behind his back and began to pace. "I put out a bulletin for the pair using their description. But it would really help to have a vehicle."

"That's probably why they left the rental here," Connor put in. So far, the private detective had been pretty quiet. He probably felt responsible for the failure of his plan. His quarry had slipped through the net.

Grace sank onto a chair. "Do you think Darryl pulled the main?"

"It seems that way," Spencer said. "And while Daria was distracting the officer, Darryl made the switch with the instrument cases. Then off they went."

"Is there anything in their rooms?" Grace leaned back in the chair, suddenly overcome with exhaustion. What a night. And she had a feeling it was far from over.

"Nothing." Connor sounded disgusted. "Clean as a whistle. They didn't even leave trash."

Speaking of trash, the balled-up letter Winston had found came to mind. *I pray you can forgive.* If Daria had written it, was she asking forgiveness of one of their victims? Grace still found it hard to believe that Daria was a hardened criminal. Maybe Grace could be a bit naive and tended to give most people the benefit of the doubt, but she wasn't that bad a judge of character. Right?

The captain's voice interrupted Grace's musing. "I'd like to talk to Alexis. Can you please bring her in here?"

"Of course." Grace pushed herself off the chair. She really ought to change her shoes. Her heels were starting to pinch. "I'll bring in a tray of coffee and cookies too."

"That would be much appreciated," Daley said. "Dinner was excellent, but I burned it off ages ago."

In the kitchen, Charlotte and her helpers were putting away food while Alexis sipped coffee and watched.

Grace studied the young woman, not sure how to broach the topic of her sister and the deep trouble she was in.

"We're almost done here," Charlotte told Grace. As Stephanie began loading the dishwasher, she made a shooing motion. "Please don't bother. It's late. I'll take care of that."

"All right, we'll get going," Stephanie said. She turned to her companion. "Ready?"

"I am," the other woman said, taking off her apron.

"I'll walk you out," Charlotte said. She glanced over her shoulder at Grace, a clear message that she was leaving on purpose to give Grace and Alexis privacy.

Grace inhaled a deep breath and squared her shoulders, gathering her courage. She sat on a stool next to Alexis. "I have some hard news to share, I'm afraid."

Alexis set her mug down, fear springing into her eyes. "About Daria? What's that snake Darryl done now?"

Her lack of illusions about her brother made it a tiny bit easier. Grace weighed her words carefully. It wouldn't be wise to make blunt accusations, not at this point. "You were right. Daria has been staying here. But she and Darryl left a short while ago."

"Where did they go?" Alexis slid off the stool, poised as though to give chase. "I'm worried about her. She needs to get away from him."

Grace couldn't agree more. "We're not sure. But the police are here, and the captain would like to talk to you."

"The police?" The young woman's face went slack with confusion. "Is Daria in trouble?"

Grace searched for a tactful yet truthful answer. "Not yet. But some things are missing. And the police think Daria and Darryl might know where they are."

Alexis stamped a foot. "I can read between the lines, you know. You think they were stealing." She narrowed her eyes. "That wouldn't be a surprise to anyone who knows my brother. He's an ex-con."

Exhausted by the stressful evening, Grace didn't think anything could give her a jolt. But this news did. Her mind hummed with questions, but she knew she'd better leave them to Daley. "Captain Daley is going to want to hear this." Grace got off the stool. "Let me put some coffee and cookies on a tray, and I'll take you to see him."

The back door opened, and Charlotte dashed into the kitchen. "Someone stole Stephanie's car!"

Stephanie and the other woman were right behind her.

"Yep, it's gone." Stephanie burst into tears. "Now what am I going to do?"

Charlotte patted the woman's shoulder. "We'll figure it out. I'll run you ladies home in a few minutes."

"But before you go," Grace said, "the police are going to want to hear about this." Now they'd have a vehicle to add to their bulletin.

Daley sent Officer Holmes to the kitchen to take Stephanie's statement, then prepared to interview Alexis in the music room. He pulled Grace aside. "Why don't you stay and listen?" he suggested. "She seems to trust you. And maybe she can stay here tonight too. I don't want to let her out of our sight until we locate her siblings."

Grace could put her in the Dogwood Suite, where Daria had been staying. "I'll have Winnie make up a room if you're done searching them."

"We are," he said. "We took fingerprints, but there wasn't anything else to gather as far as evidence goes. They must have been planning their escape for days."

After Grace spoke to Winnie, she joined the others in the music room. All the guests and musicians had been released and had left, with no sign of the runaway pair or the mandolin. It was looking extremely likely that they had stolen Stephanie's Honda sedan along with the mandolin.

Grace prayed they'd retrieve the car and the vintage instrument. The mandolin was irreplaceable, which was tragic for Jerzy. And to be practical, she had to think about the inn. Their insurance would cover it, but what a blot on their record. The insurance company might drop them, and who knew what the hit would be to their reputation?

She must have groaned aloud, because Spencer, seated nearby, sent her a concerned glance. "It's not over yet," he said in a low voice. "Keep the faith."

Daley sat in a chair across from Alexis. "All right, Miss Hargreaves. I'm Captain Keith Daley." His smile was kind.

Alexis leaned back and crossed her legs, acting casual. But Grace could tell by the tension on her face that she was petrified. "Are you going to find my sister?" Alexis asked.

"I hope so." He cleared his throat. "Any idea where she might be?"

Alexis shrugged. "She might have gone to our apartment in Chattanooga."

The captain's eyes brightened as he took out a notepad and a pen. "What's the address?"

Alexis told him. "I went there first. After I got out of the hospital."

Daley jotted down the address, then raised his brows. "Hospital?"

The young woman studied her laced fingers. "Yeah. Daria and I were in a car accident last winter. We were both in the hospital for a while, me longer than her. That's when Darryl came back into our lives." Her lip curled into almost a snarl.

"You don't like Darryl," the captain said. It wasn't a question.

"What's to like? We haven't seen him since we were, oh, three years old. Back when he got in trouble for armed robbery. But after Daria got mentioned in a couple of newspapers for her singing, he comes waltzing back."

Daley took notes. Grace figured the police would delve into Darryl's criminal background.

"So what brought you to Magnolia Harbor?" By the alertness in the captain's posture if not his words, Grace guessed he was wondering how much Alexis knew about the thieving duo.

"After I was released from the hospital, I went back to the apartment," Alexis replied. "She wasn't there, but I found a list of singing engagements. Magnolia Harbor was the next one, so I came down." She shuddered. "I was waiting for a chance to catch her alone because I didn't want to run into Darryl. When it didn't happen, I decided to come to the inn tonight, since they were supposed to leave tomorrow."

If it were up to Grace, she'd vote that Alexis didn't know about the thefts. And she was also justifiably leery of Darryl and his intentions. Her gaze met Spencer's, and she could tell that he agreed with her assessment. He was really good at silent communication, at least with her.

"You know where they were headed after this?" Daley asked.

"No, I don't," Alexis answered. "Magnolia Harbor was the last stop on the list I saw."

The captain studied the young woman for another minute before he sighed and said, "That's all for now. But I'd like you to stay in Magnolia Harbor for the time being. Mrs. Porter has offered to put you up."

Alexis whipped her head around. "You don't need to do that. I have a room." Then her face relaxed into a smile, the first Grace had seen. "But this place is much nicer. So yes, I'll stay here. Thank you."

Connor ended up staying over too. Grace gave him Darryl's room, the Buttercup Suite. She thought he needed to be at command post central, as she was dubbing the inn.

Winnie went home, and the police finally left, with promises that they would be tracking the fugitives.

Only Spencer remained after Grace shut the door on the last officer and locked it. She leaned against the door with a sigh. "What a night."

His eyes were sympathetic. "I'll say. It's well after midnight."

Grace glanced up the staircase. All was quiet. The guests had turned in, including Karen, Luke, and Osgood. Everyone had been wonderful tonight, pitching in to help get the main rooms back in shape. All while the police were crawling everywhere, carrying out their investigation. They'd certainly never forget their stay at Magnolia Harbor Inn.

"Want a mug of hot cocoa?" she asked Spencer. "I'm having one before I head to bed."

"Sure. That sounds nice." He fell into step beside her as they ambled to the kitchen. "Tonight goes in the category of truth is stranger than fiction."

Grace snorted a laugh. "Tell me about it. I almost fainted when I saw Alexis at the back door. I had no idea Daria had a twin."

Before going to her room, Karen had mentioned that she knew about Alexis. Daria had been worried about her sister's injuries after the accident. She'd even believed Alexis might have died because Darryl told her that she had.

Grace felt her teeth clench at the memory. What a cruel person Darryl Hargreaves was. Wasn't it enough that he was riding Daria's coattails, since her singing gave them access to wealthy patrons? Another result of tonight was that Luke and Julep had both filed reports about their missing personal items. The delay was a testimony of their reluctance to believe that thieves had targeted Magnolia Harbor.

Like Spencer said, truth was sometimes stranger than fiction.

And she hoped this true-crime tale would have a happy ending.

22

Daria

The stolen truck roared through the inky darkness, water swishing under its huge tires. After abandoning the stolen Honda sedan, Darryl had hot-wired this powerful but far from luxurious ride.

Daria leaned against the passenger door, trying to get as far from her brother as possible. She sure hoped the latch was still sturdy on this rusty old truck, but part of her didn't care. Her life was over. She was a fugitive from the law. She had no idea what would happen next. It felt like the future was a black tunnel with no light at the end of it.

Kind of like this dark road. On either side of the bumpy lane full of potholes, trees pressed close. Soon after Darryl had veered off the main highway, they left civilization and plunged into the wilds of South Carolina.

"Stop and let me go," she called to Darryl over the throaty engine. Even though she would be stranded and alone in the middle of nowhere, it was preferable to this. "You promised."

He chuckled, the faint light from the dashboard highlighting his features so he looked evil. "You're not going anywhere right now. I wasn't planning to have to make such a big splash, but there were cops at the inn. Even in their dinner jackets, I spotted them."

Daria had too. Well, one of the officers at least. She recognized him from the park when he'd approached her out of concern. Now she wondered if he'd been tailing her. But she'd done her part, kept him distracted while Darryl carried out the theft.

She'd had no idea Darryl was after an instrument this time. The mandolin riding behind the seat was worth more than $200,000. It was a big score, as Darryl said.

"Speaking of cops . . ." Darryl glanced at her. "Was that your doing? Did you set up a sting to get me?"

"What do you mean? I was as surprised as you to see them there." Daria gave him her best scowl. She needed him to believe that she wouldn't ever rat him out. But of course she would, if she had the chance. Then she'd confess and take her punishment.

Surprisingly, the thought of coming clean made her feel peaceful instead of scared. She touched her pocket, where the tiny Bible Winnie had given her rested. Just the reminder gave her strength.

I want to do the right thing, Lord, she prayed silently. *Please give me the opportunity.* She knew all about foxhole prayers, so she promised Him that this wasn't one of those. No, she'd walk the straight and narrow for the rest of her life and be grateful for the opportunity. Should one be granted.

"Besides," she continued, eager to stop him from thinking that she'd called the cops, "they all live in that town. They just happened to be there, listening to the music."

He scoffed. "Go ahead and tell yourself that. Most cops I know can't tell Beethoven from bluegrass."

That was unfair, but Daria bit her lip and didn't answer. The officer she'd talked to had seemed really nice and caring. But maybe it was an act. Good cop, right?

"No, something was definitely up." Darryl furrowed his brow. "Now that I look back . . . I should have known." He pressed the gas, sending them racing down the winding road. They took a tight corner at high speed. Darryl whooped when they made it around and headed into a straightaway.

Horror drenched Daria in cold sweat. She clutched the door handle, squeezing her eyes tightly shut. If they were going to crash, to roll and burn, she didn't want to see it. "Slow down!" she shouted.

His response was to drive even faster.

Daria moaned, the memory of the terrible accident with her sister breaking through a barrier in her mind.

Once again, she was with Alexis in the car on mountain roads covered with slush, snow, and black ice. They were moving too fast, the wheels were spinning, losing traction, the rear end fishtailing. Again and again they swerved, each rotation threatening to send them into a spin.

The concrete barrier, gray like the road and the winter dusk, loomed out of nowhere. Screams. A rending crunch and a shriek of metal. Then silence, a terrible silence, except for the ticking of sleet against the broken windshield.

Turning her head, which hurt so, so much. The trickle of blood running down her face.

Alexis lay slumped over the wheel.

Daria gasped and opened her eyes. Darryl was taking another hairpin turn at high speed, but she hardly noticed. She was lost in her vision of the past, the day she and Alexis had their accident.

Then the realization hit her. All this time, Daria had believed that she had been driving. But Alexis had been. It was Alexis who wouldn't slow down, Alexis who laughed at the idea of black ice making them lose control.

And this loathsome half brother of hers was being reckless on the roads tonight. "Slow down!" she yelled again. "If you don't care about me, think of the mandolin. If we crash, it'll get wrecked."

Darryl lifted his foot from the gas with a grin. "Scare you, did I? Oh, that's right, you had yourself a little accident a while ago. Are you afraid of a big old bad truck going fast?" This last was spoken in obnoxious baby talk.

"I can't believe you're related to me by blood," she said, fury making her grind out the words. "You'd think you'd care about me at least a little bit."

He mocked her with wide eyes and hoots of derision. "Maybe because I'm not your half brother."

Daria gaped at him. "What are you talking about?"

"The real Darryl is dead." He patted his chest. "I'm an old friend of his."

The air left Daria's body, exactly like the time she'd had the wind knocked out of her. She hugged herself, gasping for air, unable to catch her breath. *Darryl is dead.* Not that she'd ever loved him or even known him well. She'd been a toddler the last time she'd seen him, with a vague memory of a deep voice and a masculine figure looming over her and Alexis playing on the floor.

Now all the little pieces that hadn't added up before fell into place. Darryl claimed not to remember certain things about Grammy, his own grandmother, or other relatives. He didn't resemble Daddy or his side of the family at all. She'd attributed the confusion to a long period apart and her faulty memory.

"Did you kill him?" She spat the words. "Whoever you are."

"What? Surely you don't think I'm a murderer." His tone was derisive. "No, good old Darryl crossed the wrong people. I have no idea where he is exactly, only that he's not among the living."

"You disgust me." Daria crossed her arms and glared. "You waltz in while I'm lying in a hospital bed and claim to be my long-lost brother."

And worse, she'd fallen for it, so grateful that they hadn't been severely injured and alone. Only later, once she'd caught Darryl with a stolen wallet, did she realize that she'd made a bad bargain, agreeing to let him be her accompanist. Then he'd deftly used her worry, fear, and guilt about Alexis to manipulate her.

Instead of revealing remorse, Darryl's expression was gloating. "Pretty good trick, wasn't it? You swallowed the bait hook, line, and sinker."

"I'm glad you're not really Darryl. I'd be ashamed to claim you as a relative." She turned toward the dark landscape zipping past. She didn't want to give him the satisfaction of asking him for his real name.

"Ouch. I'm so hurt." His sardonic laughter rang out.

They continued to drive through the night.

Daria found herself clutching the small Bible and praying. *Please, God, help me. Get me out of this alive.*

23

Karen

When the lights went out, Karen thought it was kind of exciting.

The resourceful Luke switched on his cell phone flashlight and put his arm around her in a most cozy manner. Lightning flashed and thunder rumbled as he guided her to a seat, increasing the sense of a cozy adventure.

"I guess we'd better wait on dessert," Luke remarked. "We need to see what we're eating."

That was fine with her, sitting squashed with him on a love seat in the corner.

After their initial alarm, the other guests were laughing as they lit candles or turned on flashlight apps. Karen glanced out the tall windows. Rain was starting to come down hard. The outage must be related to the storm.

Someone shouted, followed by a shrill whistle cutting through the noisy chatter.

"What's going on?" Karen asked.

Around them, other people were asking the same question. Then the news reached them, relayed from person to person. Jerzy Flynn's mandolin was missing.

Luke put his hand on his wrist. "The thief strikes again."

Luke's watch. Julep's necklace. Now a valuable instrument. "Who is doing this?" Karen cried. "It's awful."

From the angry muttering around her, she guessed others felt the same way.

"Wait here," Luke said. "I'll see if I can find out what's going on." He navigated through the crowd and was soon out of sight.

Meanwhile, Karen's mind ticked over the possibilities. It had to be the same person who was stealing. Daria's earlier words came to mind. *Thank you for everything. You've been more wonderful than you know.* That sounded like a farewell. But Daria wasn't scheduled to check out until tomorrow. And she'd been so upset. Was it about her sister or something else?

The lights came back on, and the others clapped and cheered. People turned off their cell phone lights with sheepish laughs. Many of them approached the dessert table and started to dig into the delectable display of ice cream and toppings.

Karen stood, ready to go find Luke. But then she saw him threading through the tightly packed bodies toward her. She smiled and waved to let him know she was still in the same place.

"You'll never believe it," he whispered when he reached her side. "Daria and Darryl took off. The police think they stole the mandolin."

The news hit Karen in the solar plexus. *Daria?* "I can't believe she had anything to do with it," she said hotly. "She's my friend."

Luke put his arm around her. "I know how you feel. It's really upsetting. Maybe they're wrong. But listen, shall I get you some ice cream? Then I'm going to file a report about my watch. I'm pretty certain now that it's not misplaced."

Karen sank onto the love seat. "Just a little bowl, okay?" She remembered the flavors from the placards. "How about vanilla bean, Mexican chocolate, and espresso granita? A taste of each." She wasn't really sure she'd be able to enjoy dessert right now, but after all Charlotte's trouble, she should at least taste it.

Julep sat beside her. "Have you heard the news?" Frown lines bracketed the older woman's mouth and creased her brow. "I can't believe it." She put a hand to her chest as though remembering her stolen necklace.

"Me neither," Karen said. "I really like Daria. There's something sweet and vulnerable about her."

"That's what I thought. She visited me in my home, you know." Julep snorted gently. "Along with her no-good brother. I'll bet he's behind all this."

Karen wasn't one to rush to judgment, but yes, she'd be happy to blame everything on Darryl. He was a creep. "Something happened to her sister," she said tentatively. She was leery about breaking a confidence, but she trusted Julep somehow. The woman practically radiated good sense and integrity. "I think Darryl might be holding something over her head."

That made sense. He certainly was using her sister to torture her. So blackmail sounded like par for the course.

Luke appeared in front of them. He gave a dish of ice cream and a napkin to Karen, then asked Julep, "Would you like something?"

Julep peeked at the bowl. "Maybe a little vanilla bean, if you don't mind. Thank you."

As Luke strode away on his errand, Julep said, "He's a nice young man. A real keeper."

Karen almost choked on a spoonful of ice cream. She put the napkin to her lips and swallowed. "Oh, Julep. We've just started dating."

Julep patted Karen's knee, the diamonds in her rings flashing. "Sometimes one date is all it takes. When it's right, you know. And when it's wrong, no amount of time can fix it."

Karen realized that was a very good description of her relationship with Joshua. "Thanks. You clarified something for me."

The older woman seemed pleased. "Glad I can be of help."

Luke returned and handed Julep a bowl of ice cream.

"Thank you, my dear," Julep said as she accepted the dessert.

"I'm going to file a police report," Luke said. "Julep, have you done that yet?"

Julep touched her chest again, sighing. "No, but I suppose I should. I need to for my insurance. And Dean's insurance. I'd rather get my necklace back than get money for it, though."

"Maybe you will," Karen said. "If they catch the thief."

"Let's pray they do, sugar." Julep sounded sad. "And that Daria is all right."

At around one o'clock in the morning, someone tapped lightly on Karen's door.

Despite being exhausted, she was only half asleep, the evening's events playing in her head over and over like a waking dream. She thought of the upset of the mandolin theft, Daria's suspicious disappearance, and the amazing arrival of Alexis, her twin. Karen had been relieved to see that Alexis was healthy and whole, recovered from her injuries for the most part.

The tapping continued.

Karen rolled out of bed and tiptoed to the door, her heart beginning to pound. Maybe Daria had come back. That thought woke her up. "Daria?" she asked.

"No, it's me, Alexis." A pause. "I have something I need to show you."

Karen had been honored that Daria's sister seemed to trust her. After the police had finally left, they'd chatted in the Dogwood Suite for a few minutes. Alexis confided that she was an artist too and was planning to go to art school. So they'd talked about art, and they had made a date to go sketching. Maybe that would help them stop worrying about Daria for a little while.

Karen opened the door. "Come in." She stepped over to the wall and flipped on the overhead light switch, squinting at the sudden brightness.

Alexis shuffled inside the room. Her feet were bare, and she wore a baggy T-shirt and yoga pants borrowed from the taller Karen, since her own nightclothes were still in the motel room she'd rented across town. She held an open magazine in her hands. "This was in Daria's room."

Karen glanced at the publication. It was a tourist guide to South Carolina. The inn stocked the suites with such literature for guests.

Alexis set the magazine on the bureau and pointed to a map with one delicate finger. "I think this might be where Darryl and Daria are headed."

Karen moved closer and saw that she was pointing to a tiny lake near the North Carolina border. More of a pond, really. "Have you been there before?"

"No, but I heard about the place from my grammy. One of my cousins owns a cabin there. Apparently, it's really isolated, which means it's an ideal place to hide out." Her blue eyes, so like Daria's, shone with excitement. She jabbed at the page. "And look. Someone circled the pond with a pen."

A burst of energy rippled through Karen. She was ready for action, reckless though it might be. "Let's go see if they're there. And if they are, we'll let the police know, since this might be a wild-goose chase."

"I sure hope it isn't," Alexis said. "What do you have for a car? I understand the roads are pretty rough up there."

Karen's momentum flagged briefly. She'd rented a small sedan, but she knew someone who had an SUV. "We need to talk to Luke." Maybe they could borrow his vehicle.

They rushed to his room and knocked.

After they filled Luke in, he insisted on going with them. "We really need another person," he said, smoothing his sleep-disheveled hair. "Which room is Connor Benton in?"

Within ten minutes, the foursome was in Luke's SUV and on the road. Karen had left the innkeepers a note on the front counter, realizing that if they were delayed getting back, the women would worry. It wasn't every day that four guests left the inn in the middle of the night.

Luke was at the wheel, and Alexis was in the passenger seat navigating. Connor and Karen sat in the back.

After they'd been on the road awhile and were well north of Magnolia Harbor, Luke yawned. "Who wants coffee? I know I do."

"We'd better get you some," Karen said with a laugh. "No sleeping at the wheel."

"I could use a doughnut," Connor said. "Stakeouts always require sugar."

Karen was glad Luke suggested that Connor come along. The private detective was most likely experienced in covert operations and tracking people down.

An all-night gas station appeared ahead, and Luke pulled in at one of the pumps. "I'm going to fill up. Why don't you all get the snacks?" He told Karen how he wanted his coffee, then began pumping gas.

Inside the store, the clerk watched with bleary eyes as they entered. "You know what?" he said. "Some jerk stole my truck tonight."

Connor placed a box of doughnuts on the counter, his tired eyes suddenly alert. "When was this?"

The clerk rubbed his scruffy jaw. "Around midnight. I went out to get something, and it was gone. He took the truck and left me a little Honda."

Karen exchanged excited glances with the others. Darryl must have decided to switch vehicles. "That's awful," she said, injecting dismay into her voice. "Who would do such a thing?" She'd guessed the clerk was seeking sympathy by sharing the story, rather than expecting them to do something about the theft.

The clerk's smile was gratified. "I know, right? That truck is my pride and joy."

"What does it look like?" Connor asked.

The clerk launched into a lengthy description of his stolen truck.

"It sounds great," Connor remarked after the clerk finished. "I sure hope you reported it to the police."

"Yeah, I did. They came by already and took a statement." His expression was glum. "Let's just hope I get it back in one piece."

They echoed this hope. After purchasing tall cups of coffee—made fresh, according to the clerk—and bottled water, chips, and doughnuts, they climbed back into the SUV.

"We're searching for a green Ford pickup," Connor told Luke. He gave him the year and model. "It has a truck cap, monster tires, and a light rack on the cab."

"Darryl swapped the Honda for the store clerk's truck," Karen explained.

"Good call on his part," Alexis put in. "Probably figured they needed it to get to the cabin."

"Maybe so," Luke said, starting the engine. "We now know two things. They came this way, and they're driving a pickup. We're on the right track."

After another hour of driving, Karen was glad for that glimmer of certainty. Judging by the remote, forested countryside, they were heading deep into the middle of nowhere. The road was winding and narrow and in bad condition, requiring that Luke drive slowly.

Now and then, Alexis brightened the screen on Luke's phone to be sure they were still headed the right way. GPS wasn't any use out here on unnamed roads, but she'd found a detailed map of the area.

"Go slow," Alexis warned. "Look for a dirt road on our right."

They missed it the first time, only realizing their mistake when the road started to go uphill again. So Luke had to find a place to turn around.

They crawled along the road, stopping a few times to see if an opening was the actual road or a driveway or an old logging cut. Finally, they found it, a barely passable track through thick trees and brush. The SUV bucked and swayed over potholes and rocks.

"I don't think your cousin comes out here very often," Connor commented.

"He's been suffering from health problems for the past several years," Alexis said. She held up a hand. "We'd better stop here. If we go any farther, they might hear the engine."

"Good point," Luke said. He backed the vehicle into a clearing, ready for a quick escape.

They slid out of the vehicle, careful not to slam the doors. They used cell phone flashlights since they provided only a pencil beam of light, but Luke brought along a big, heavy flashlight, just in case. And Connor had the gun he was licensed to carry.

As they crept down the dirt road, Karen shivered with excitement. The night air was damp and cool under the thick trees. A chorus of tree frogs accompanied them, and overhead, the clouds were breaking apart to reveal stars.

She felt alive and alert to her tingling fingertips, the depression and anxiety having lifted like the mist after the rain.

"Doing okay?" Luke whispered. He was walking in the lead, Karen right behind him. Then came Alexis, with Connor bringing up the rear.

"I'm great," Karen whispered back. "I know I should be petrified, but I'm not." For one thing, she was taking action, instead of reacting to circumstances beyond her control. Now the events in Africa seemed like a tidal wave that had washed over her, leaving her drifting and rudderless.

Luke put a finger to his mouth to indicate that they were drawing close and needed to be extra quiet.

The cabin lay in a little hollow surrounded by tall trees. Lights shone in the two windows they could see. The structure was small, probably only one big room and a bedroom, Karen guessed.

When they almost reached the end of the driveway, Luke led them into the bracken and across the ground strewn with pine needles. Under the shelter of a huge tree, he stopped them. "I'm going to peek into the window and get the lay of the land."

"I'm going with you," Connor said.

The men walked down to the cabin. The rear window apparently didn't reveal much, so they went around the side of the house.

"I'm not waiting here," Alexis said. "She's my sister."

Before Karen could object, Alexis marched toward the cabin.

There was nothing else to do but follow. Between where they were standing and the cabin was a minefield of junk. Karen almost fell when she tripped on an ancient roll of wire next to the old metal bed frame she was skirting.

In the light filtering out from the cabin, Karen plainly saw Luke rolling his eyes when they showed up. But he didn't object when Karen and Alexis moved closer to peer inside.

Karen bit back a gasp. Darryl had tied Daria to a chair and was pacing back and forth in front of her, waving a revolver in the air. The window was cracked at the bottom, so she moved even closer to listen.

"This is your last chance to cooperate. If you don't, I'll leave you here to rot for a few days until I'm south of the border and safe with my buddy." His smile was nasty. "And maybe a little while after that."

"I'm not leaving the States," Daria said. "My whole life is here.

My sister is here."

"But your sister—"

"No!" Daria shouted. "My sister is not dead. Stop telling me that."

Karen felt Alexis flinch. She put a hand on her arm to restrain her.

Alexis groaned. "I'm gonna kill him." She jerked away from Karen's grip.

"No, wait," Karen said. An idea dropped whole into her mind. It was inspired by a memory from Africa when she watched men and boys hunt in the bush. "I have an idea." Tugging on Alexis's arm, she walked back to where the men were standing.

As a group, they moved farther away so they could confer without being overheard.

"I don't want to rush the house," Luke said. "He might shoot Daria or one of us by accident."

"That's a very good point," Connor said. "I thought of that too, since I'm armed. But it's too dicey." He took out his phone and sent a text. "I'm letting the police know where we are and what the situation is like."

"We could disable the truck so he's stuck here," Alexis suggested.

Inside the cabin, Darryl shouted, and then Daria screamed.

Alexis clenched her fists. "Or you could let me have at him." She sounded fierce.

Karen took a deep breath. "When I was in Africa . . ." She told them her idea.

A short while later, working fast despite being in almost total darkness, they were ready.

From the shelter of the woods, Luke lobbed a rock against the cabin door. It banged, sounding like a knock. He did it a few more times.

Darryl opened the door cautiously and poked his head out. "Who's there?" he called. When no one answered, he shrugged and went back inside.

Luke threw another rock.

Darryl opened the door and stepped onto the porch. "Cut it out." He waved the revolver around. "I'm armed. And dangerous." He took another step, and the almost invisible wire snare Karen had built closed around his ankle. Darryl went down, falling heavily like a log in the forest. The gun flew out of his hand and into the bushes.

In a flash, Connor was on the porch, pointing his firearm at the man. "Darryl Hargreaves, you are under arrest—"

Darryl opened one eye. "Two problems with that. You're not a cop, and I'm not Darryl Hargreaves."

Luke leaped up onto the porch, a length of rope at the ready. "Well, whoever you are, you aren't going anywhere. We'll let the police sort you out."

With Connor's gun in his face, Darryl allowed Luke to release his leg from the snare and then secure his hands and feet.

Alexis bolted out of the trees toward the cabin, Karen on her heels. They thumped up the steps and burst through the door.

Daria whipped her head around when she heard them come in. Her mouth dropped open, and her eyes grew huge. "Alexis?" She laughed. "Are you really here, or did I die or something?"

"Or something." Alexis dashed over to her sister and kissed the top of her head. "We're going to get you out of here." She began to work at the knots binding her sister's hands.

Joining them, Karen crouched to take care of the rope around Daria's ankles.

"I can't believe it," Daria said.

Karen glanced up and saw that Daria's eyes were full of tears.

"I thought I was a goner," Daria admitted.

"Not while we're around," Karen said stoutly. "We need a knife to cut this rope." She got up and scanned the cabin. She spotted a pocketknife on an old metal table and snatched it. "This will do."

While Karen and Alexis worked on setting Daria free, they filled her in on the events of the night.

"So you saw the magazine?" Daria asked. "I left it open to that page on purpose. And circled the pond." Free of the bonds at last, she jumped up and hugged her sister.

A siren whooped, and blue lights flashed through the cabin windows.

"Looks like the police are here," Karen said.

No doubt the Magnolia Harbor force had called the local department.

Moving a little stiffly from being tied up, Daria went to the couch. "They'll want to see this." A black duffel bag sat next to an instrument case. Daria unzipped the case and, although the light was dim, Karen saw the glitter of jewels and precious metals inside. Stolen goods. Daria stood tall. "Time for me to make a confession."

"What do you mean?" Alexis asked. "You didn't steal, did you?"

Daria shook her head, her expression sad but resolute. "I think they call it being an accessory." She reached out and brushed a gentle finger down her sister's cheek. "Don't worry. I'm doing the right thing." Light broke across her face. "And it feels really good."

Grace

The pink light of dawn tinting the sky was the excuse Grace needed to get up. She'd rolled around restlessly all night, worried about Daria and the thefts. When she did sleep, she had nightmares, the kind it was better to forget.

"Come on, boy," she said to Winston. "How about an early walk?"

He jumped out of his dog bed, tail wagging and tongue hanging out.

Grace laughed. "I wish I had your energy." She rummaged through her dresser drawers and picked out a pair of capris and a top, then headed for the shower.

When Grace and Winston entered the kitchen, Charlotte wasn't up yet, a rare event indeed. As the morning sun strengthened, beaming through the big windows, Grace put on coffee and took a coffee cake out to defrost.

After she filled a large travel mug with coffee, she opened the back door and stepped into the beautiful day with Winston at her side. Droplets from the previous night's storm glittered on the leaves and flowers and in the grass. Since the grass was so wet, Grace decided to stay on the path. That led them around to the front, and to her surprise, she noticed Luke's SUV pulling into the parking area.

She waved in greeting, mildly curious why he was out and about so early. Then all four doors opened, and Karen, Alexis, and Connor piled out too. Now she *had* to find out what was going on. She and Winston walked to meet the group, Winston sniffing at everyone's shoes.

"Good morning," Luke said. He had dark shadows under his eyes, and he needed a shave. "We've had quite an adventure."

"We found Daria and Darryl," Karen announced. "Only his name is Bart Griggs."

"He's a career criminal." Alexis wrinkled her nose. "Not our half brother."

"The police are questioning them both now," Luke said.

"And we recovered my clients' jewelry, along with Luke's watch," Connor added.

Grace held up her mug. "Hold on. I'm going to need more coffee before I hear the rest of this. Let's go in, and then please take it from the top."

In the kitchen, the guests sat at the bar while Grace poured cups of coffee. "Is anyone hungry?" She could fry an egg almost as skillfully as Charlotte.

A chorus of yeses met her question.

While Grace cracked eggs into a bowl for scrambling, bacon already frying, Karen started to explain. She told Grace how Alexis had spotted Daria's clue.

"Once I thought about it, I knew I'd heard of that pond before," Alexis said. "One of my cousins owns a cabin there."

"Then they woke me up," Luke said. "They wanted to borrow my car, but I wasn't going to miss out."

"And to think I didn't hear a thing." Grace poured creamy yellow liquid into a hot frying pan and began to stir the mixture. She adjusted the heat so the eggs wouldn't cook too fast.

The back door opened, and soft singing announced the arrival of Charlotte. She stopped in her tracks when she saw the group already in the kitchen. "Aren't you all a bunch of early risers?" she said with a laugh.

"You're just in time to hear the story," Grace said. "They've been up all night on an adventure."

Charlotte tied on an apron. "Sounds interesting." She inspected the eggs Grace was making, then gently nudged her sister aside. "Want to do the toast?"

"I can take a hint," Grace said with good humor. She went over to the toaster and began untying a loaf of bakery bread from Hanson's.

Luke picked up the tale where they'd left off. "So I suggested we bring Connor along, as backup and for his expertise. With Alexis navigating, we headed out."

Between the four, they relayed finding out Darryl—Bart—had stolen a truck and how they tracked them to the cabin deep in the woods.

"We overheard Bart saying that he was heading south of the border," Connor said. "People can disappear in Mexico, Central America, and the islands. They recently extradited a guy who'd been in Mexico for more than thirty years. So we got there in the nick of time."

Charlotte removed the fluffy eggs from the heat. "I need to call Dean and tell him the good news. But I'm sure he's not up yet." She set out plates and divided the eggs onto the plates. Then she used tongs to place the bacon next to the eggs.

Grace buttered the pieces of toast and added them to the plates.

"He roped my sister into his evil plan," Alexis said, her voice dripping with disgust. "Using me as leverage."

Grace gently broached what she knew was a delicate subject. "What do you think will happen with Daria?"

Alexis traced a finger along the countertop. "I'm not sure. She definitely needs a good attorney." Tears pooled in her eyes. "But she was so brave. She marched out of the cabin and turned herself in."

Karen put an arm around Alexis. "We'll figure it out. You have friends now."

"You certainly do," Grace said. "And I'll make a call once it's a civil hour." Julep Buckley's son was an attorney in Charleston. She wasn't sure what he did in his practice, but at the least he could give Daria a referral.

"You'd do that for Daria?" Alexis sounded disbelieving. "What is this place? You're so wonderful."

Karen patted her on the back. "You're right. There's something special about Magnolia Harbor Inn. We've all experienced it."

Karen

Karen considered her own words later that day after she took a long nap. There *was* something special about the inn, something healing and comforting. She thought back to the broken, weary, ill person she had been when she arrived. Now she was almost fully restored to her old self.

Emma called right after Karen got out of the shower. "I thought I'd check in on you to see how your week went," her sister said.

Karen sat, still wrapped in her towel, and rummaged through her suitcase for something to wear. She planned to go kayaking with Luke before the social hour. Thankfully, today was much cooler after the storms had blown through.

Where to begin? She decided not to tell her sister about the events of the previous night. Emma would think she'd gone off the deep end, chasing after a criminal in the woods. So she contented herself with the more personal.

"I'm doing really well. I've gotten a chance to rest here." *Among other things.* She paused. "And guess what? I'm painting again."

"You are?" Emma said. She sounded delighted. "Paint me something, okay?" A request like that was so typical of her.

In the past, Karen had immediately felt obligated. But now she refused to promise anything until she was ready. She was never returning to an overcommitted, overstressed life. "I'm still getting back in the groove, but I will once I get my feet wet again." Karen found a pair of shorts and put them on. "Speaking of wet feet, I've also been doing a lot of kayaking. In fact, I'm going out in a few minutes."

"That sounds like fun," Emma said, a wistful tone in her voice. "There's a nice lake there, right? We're sweltering up here. Hot and humid, rinse and repeat."

"Let's go, just you and me, when I get home. You'll love it." Karen hesitated. Should she mention Luke? It really was so new... She decided to go for it. "And guess what? I'm dating someone."

Emma squealed into the phone. "Tell me more. I can't believe you met someone there. I thought maybe it would be all older people, like that cruise I went on."

Karen remembered that cruise. Emma and a girlfriend had been the only two people under sixty on board, which was very disappointing for them at the time.

"People of all ages stay here. Luke is an astronomy professor." Karen gave her sister a few more details, enough to satisfy her for now. "I'll send a picture later," she added before Emma could ask.

Emma exhaled loudly. "I am so, so happy for you. Whatever happens with Luke, I'm glad you're moving on. Now that it's over, well, I have to tell you, I never liked Joshua."

Karen barked a laugh. "Seriously? You're saying that now? Please feel free to tell me what you think. I had reservations too, and maybe I would have paid more attention to them."

Her sister was actually stunned into silence, which was rare. After a minute, she said, a humble note in her voice, "Okay, I'll do that. I know I'm opinionated, and I've been trying to cut back on that."

"I love you, Emma. Right now, I have to go meet Luke. But let's talk tomorrow before I check out."

"Sounds good," Emma said. In the background, children's

voices and barking could be heard. "The gang's back, so I've got to go anyway. Love you too."

Karen smiled as she disconnected. Getting away had been refreshing, but now she was eager to go home and see her family. She'd gotten an e-mail that her agency had remote office positions available, which meant she could help fight malaria without being on the front lines. Emma also had a lead on an apartment—and a friend who gave art lessons. She was so blessed to have supportive people in her life.

And Luke? Frankly, whenever she thought of him, she felt all sparkly inside, fizzing like a July sparkler. For now, they'd have a long-distance relationship, but working remotely would allow her to visit him frequently. She had every confidence that they'd figure it out as they went along.

She put on her water sandals, grabbed her key, and hurried out the door.

Luke met her down at the dock, where he already had the kayaks in the water and life jackets and paddles ready. He still appeared tired but a hundred times better than earlier. Without saying much, they got into the boats and paddled along the shore. The late afternoon sun slanted across the water and land, the huge oaks casting long, dark shadows.

Up on the inn veranda, two identical blonde women sat in rockers. Karen realized that Daria was back. A burst of gladness caused her to lift her paddle with a shout. She waved at the sisters, and they waved back.

"I heard they released Daria," Luke said. "Julep's son is representing her."

"That's good news," Karen said. "I pray everything goes well for her."

"Me too." He grinned as he flicked droplets of water at her with his paddle.

She shrieked in mock dismay at the splashing.

"Race you," he called.

Smiling, Karen dug her paddle into the water and sent her boat gliding ahead. She gave an exultant yell, which echoed around the lake and scared a couple of ducks into flapping away.

A new adventure had begun.

26

Daria

Her heart glowing with warmth, Daria waved at Karen, who was paddling past. Daria had a feeling they would be friends forever. Some people were like that, meant to be in your life, come what may.

A giggle rose to her lips, perhaps a strange reaction for someone in so much trouble. But the events of the last couple of days felt exactly like jumping off a steep cliff only to be caught in gentle arms.

Julep had hired her an attorney—her son, who was extremely well-regarded and influential with judges. Grace had said that Daria and Alexis could stay a few more days while Winnie lined up an apartment for them. Daria even had a job, singing at The Tidewater on weekends.

And best of all, she had her sister back.

Daria grinned, barely able to contain her joy. "I'm about ready to bust. I really thought you were . . . you know." She couldn't bring herself to repeat Darryl's lie about Alexis being dead. "I feel like my life has been restored, that I've been given a second chance."

"That's because you have," the more practical Alexis said. "And me too. I'm never going to drive like a reckless fool again. And other things."

Daria felt in her pocket and pulled out the small Bible. "Remember how Grammy used to read the Bible to us? I think we should do it together again. It was when we stopped that we got off track." She rocked slowly, waiting for a reaction, not wanting her sister to feel coerced.

"We can do that," Alexis said at last. "I always liked Psalms." She smiled at her sister. "They're songs, right?"

"They are. Worship songs written by David, for the most part." Daria leafed through the Bible, searching for that section.

"I've been writing songs," Alexis said. "Even though we're twins, I'm not such a great singer, as you know. But I'm not bad at stringing words together."

Daria stopped rocking. "You're a great writer. I'd love to see what you came up with."

Now Alexis fished around in her pocket. "It's my dream that you sing songs written by me. Wouldn't that be cool?"

"Very cool." Daria took the page of lyrics. "I'm excited to read this. But right now, I'm going to read the first Psalm."

27

Grace

"What's on the menu for tonight's social?" Grace asked Charlotte. She went to the fridge and removed a pitcher of iced tea, then filled two glasses.

Charlotte glanced up from her tablet. "How did you know I was thirsty?" She scanned the screen. "For the social, we're having fingerling potatoes with smoked salmon and avocado, crab bites, teriyaki beef, and cheese puffs. Plus, the usual veggie platter."

"All of it sounds delicious." Grace sliced a lemon and dropped pieces into their glasses, then handed one of them to Charlotte.

"Thanks. Now that the temps are cooler, I'm cranking up the ovens, as you can see."

"That's great." Grace smiled. "I've had the best day."

"Me too," Charlotte said. "I'm so happy that Jerzy got his mandolin back. And Julep, her necklace. And you get the idea." She opened the fridge and started removing ingredients.

Someone knocked on the back door.

Grace gave Charlotte a questioning look. They weren't expecting any deliveries or visitors, and Winnie was at home, spending time with Herb.

Charlotte shrugged.

"I'll get it," Grace said. All she saw through the glass was a huge, colorful bouquet. Then she saw Dean's face peeking around it. Grace smiled. Someone was going to love those. "Come on in." She stepped back so he could edge by. "Charlotte's in the kitchen."

"Where else?" Dean laughed. "It's her natural habitat." He preceded her down the short hallway.

In the kitchen, Charlotte gasped. "Those are spectacular."

Grace arrived back in the room as Dean set the flowers down on a side counter. "These are to say thank you," the restaurant owner said. "You really saved me by stepping in and making desserts this past week."

Charlotte reached out and cupped a blush rose. "No problem. You'd do the same for me, right?" She bent to inhale the sweet aroma of unfurling blossoms.

Dean turned to Grace. "They're for you too. I want to thank you for your support after Julep's necklace was stolen. I know you were dealing with the same kind of incident."

"Yes, it was one of the worst things we've experienced since opening the inn." Grace motioned toward the fridge. She still felt a rush of relief every time she remembered the ordeal was over. "Iced tea?"

"I wouldn't say no," Dean said. He glanced at the wall clock. "I've got a few minutes before I'll be needed back at The Tidewater."

After Grace poured him a glass, he sat at the counter while the sisters washed up and got to work making appetizers.

"We were just saying how relieved we are that the stolen items were recovered," Grace said as she sliced peppers for the vegetable tray.

"Me too." Dean swirled the ice cubes in his glass. "I felt horrible about Julep's necklace being lifted right under my nose. But *she* comforted *me*. Julep is amazing."

"An example of true grace under fire." Grace arranged the slices on a platter. "Her son is representing Daria. He thinks she'll probably get off with probation and community service. Julep suggested she teach singing at the inner-city camp the church sponsors every summer."

"Oh yeah? That would be great." Dean turned to watch Charlotte. "What are you making?"

Charlotte stopped cutting tiny potatoes in half and threw him a teasing look. "I don't know if I should tell you. Trade secrets and all that."

Dean pretended to twirl a mustache. "I am a spy. I plan to steal all your best recipes."

Someone else knocked on the door.

This time Dean offered to answer the summons. "Special delivery," he announced as he strode back into the room, preceding Spencer who held a huge bouquet.

"I guess I'm not the only one who had the idea," Spencer said, eyeing Dean's arrangement. His flowers were a heady mix of gardenias, orchids, and hibiscus. "Anyway, these are for you both. I figured you needed flowers after the rough week you had."

"Oh, they're wonderful." Grace darted over to dip her nose into the blooms. "We were just talking about the latest updates regarding Daria." She gave Spencer the news while pouring him a glass of tea.

While they talked, Charlotte slid the potatoes into the oven, then handed ingredients from the fridge to Grace, who set them on the counter. While Charlotte dumped fresh crabmeat into a bowl and cracked eggs, Grace grated a block of cheddar.

"Some of my former colleagues are involved in the case now," Spencer said. "Bart Griggs has some very unsavory associates. They're hoping he'll turn state's evidence."

"Poor Daria." Grace put the cheese into Charlotte's mixing bowl. "I think he's an expert manipulator. I understand she had a head injury in the crash and that made it easier for him to confuse her." She reached for a long cooking sheet and sprayed it.

Charlotte chopped fresh parsley and dumped it into her bowl. "And once she was in, she couldn't figure out how to get out." She picked up a melon baller and dropped perfect scoops of crab mixture onto the prepared tray.

Sensing eyes on her as she turned on the second oven, Grace whirled around. The men were watching her and Charlotte work with nearly identical expressions of amazed interest.

"You two make a great team," Dean said. "I wish I could get my kitchen crew to operate that smoothly."

"Lots of practice," Grace said. "Plus, she gets testy if I mess up." She opened the oven door in preparation.

Charlotte elbowed her away from the oven door, hamming it up. "Step aside. Step aside." They both laughed as Charlotte slid the appetizers inside.

Someone knocked on the back door.

"Again? Who is it this time?" Grace went to the door and opened it.

Abbott Forbes stood there, holding a large arrangement of calla lilies, lilacs, and roses, all white. His smile was shy. "I'm sorry. I went to the front, but no one was there. I hope you don't mind my coming in this way."

"Of course not. Please come in." Grace motioned to the flowers. "I'm guessing those are for Daria?"

His smile broadened. "You got it. Is she around?"

"On the back veranda. I'll take you through." Grace led the way. She'd noticed Abbott's budding interest in Daria and was glad her legal troubles seemed not to have changed that. As for Daria, Grace had no idea if she returned Abbott's feelings.

Grace opened the door to the veranda. The twins were seated in rockers, Alexis listening while Daria read to her from what looked like a small Bible. "Daria, you have company."

The young woman's expression of joy when she saw Abbott told Grace everything she needed to know.

Magnolia Harbor Inn was responsible for yet another happy ending.